POSTCARDS TO

Father

a novel **Abraham**

CATHERINE LEWIS

POSTCARDS TO

Father

a novel   Abraham

Atheneum Books for Young Readers
New York · London · Toronto · Sydney · Singapore

Image on page 289 is from an original pencil drawing
of Lincoln's feet by his master shoemaker

Atheneum Books for Young Readers
An imprint of Simon & Schuster Children's Publishing Division
1230 Avenue of the Americas
New York, New York 10020

Book design by Nina Barnett

The text of this book is set in New Baskerville.

Printed in the United States of America

10 9 8 7 6 5 4 3 2 1

Library of Congress Cataloging-in-Publication Data

Lewis, Catherine (Catherine Anne)
Postcards to Father Abraham/ by Catherine Lewis.
p. cm.
Summary: When sixteen-year-old Meghan loses her leg to
cancer and her brother to Vietnam, she expresses intense anger
in postcards which she writes to her idol, Abraham Lincoln.
ISBN 0-689-82852-7 (alk. paper)
[1. Self-acceptance Fiction. 2. Physically handicapped Fiction.
3. Lincoln, Abraham, 1809-1865 Fiction.] I. Title.
PZ7.L584743Po 2000 [Fic]-dc21 99-27005

SLJ 5/00 7-10

$10.80

$8/00

M 803

In memory of my mother
and
to my father

Acknowledgments

I would like to thank Karen Kerner, M.D., of Columbia Presbyterian Hospital, for the gift of her time and medical expertise. For reading and offering suggestions, I am indebted to Heather Henson. To my editor, Caitlyn Dlouhy, who believed in this novel from the beginning, I am deeply grateful. And lastly, thanks to Naomi Holoch, who was there every step of the way.

Contents

Prologue

*R*unning is one of the few things I know a lot about because I do it all the time. Or used to. I know my saints because of my Catholic girlhood. I know Lincoln because his breath molecules are still in the air around me. Lincoln: Honest Abe, Rail Splitter, Long Legs.

I've been to all the Lincoln sites in central Illinois, but most of the good stuff—his house, his law office, his tomb—is right here in Springfield. There's even a bank (not ours) where you can go and see his original account ledger.

Some days when I run down the old streets he used to frequent, I feel as though I've just missed him, as though his coattails had just fluttered around the corner ahead of me. A hundred-some years he's been dead and it still feels like he's everywhere in this town. In ways that would probably make him scratch his head, like the "U-Like Lincoln-Son" Chinese restaurant.

Everyone around here has a Lincoln story or two. At our house, we've even got an old leather couch called—you guessed it—the Lincoln sofa, on account of it being a million years old and in our family forever. Truth is he probably never sat on it like the Banker claims, but I like to think that he might have.

What really makes me love him, though, is a photograph. The one taken right before his Gettysburg speech. Oh, how terribly beautiful he looks. Like a man being slowly crushed to death who knows it can't be helped. The way we all feel sometimes.

I.
Bargain

Remembering

There're few places better to run than Illinois cornfields in June. The loam is soft beneath your feet. It spreads out to the sides of your shoes like water parting in a pool. Cornfields stretching far as you can see. Clean green rows. New leaves curling in the wind. Tiny stalks in June—hard to imagine them taller than Lincoln by August.

And I run. Up and down the rows of the long flat field. Half mile there. Half mile back. Feel the dirt swoosh swoosh. And the paper stalks rattling in my wake. It's the muffled sound of the crowd, cheering me on. I reach the end of the lane—breathless, my arms high in the air. I take a bow, then jog a victory lap. Feel the little pats and slaps on my legs from eager congratulators. One day they will tell their children they touched magic in motion.

So much for dreams. No magic. No miracles.

3

Doctors

The worst thing about losing my leg is that I'll never be able to run like I used to. Not down the brick paved streets or over sidewalks split open by tree roots, or across the fields.

A day before they went at it with their saws and scissors, all the Doctor Wanna-bes came in to gawk. Two of them started arguing over how much to take off. Like I wasn't even there. Just a piece of meat on the table. Meghan Hartman. The daily special.

Doctor Take More said it's better to be certain. Get all the cancer. Doctor Take Less was more conservative. What about recovery and the patient's gait?

Doctors. Read my simple list: Doctor Jekyll, Doctor Frankenstein, Doctor Mengele, Doctor Dolittle, Doctors Take More and Take Less.

Where's Killian?

4

Bargain

I sometimes wish if there was a God, she would pick me up and throw me like a baseball back to the summer of '66. I'd land on the run. Along black-top roads that lead to open spaces. Early. Before tar bubbles form. Before humidity sucks the air out of my lungs.

Afterwards, I'd grab my bike and pedal to Grass Lake. I'd cannonball off the rickety dock. Float on my back. Kick with my legs. Splash with my toes. And the jumbled mess inside of me would just drift away in the cool water.

There are moments, like the second before I fall asleep, or when I smell Coppertone or see a dragon-fly, that I find a window into time and am there all over again, cooling the sweat from a long run. Then bang, it slams shut. And there's only now, this moment, and me, the legless wonder.

In '66 I was ten. We were a picture-book family. My brother, Killian, hadn't left for Vietnam. Killian. Some nights I take his old letters out of my cigar box and hold them between my hands. Then I picture him walking through the door, a zing to his step— like in the old days.

Killian was shy and sensitive and people always took to him. Right away you noticed his long eyelashes, dark and thin like a painter's brush. The second thing you noticed were his teeth. They had an opaque quality to them like kernels of white corn. Small and tightly wedged in a row. The teeth of a little boy.

If there was a God, here's what I'd trade her to talk to Killian for just five minutes: My 45 single of "The Thrill Is Gone." A stack of vintage Beatles albums. The silver dollars my great-aunts left me. And maybe, just maybe . . . my other leg.

Killian on the Ice Pond

*O*n the shallow duck pond near our house. My little sister, PJ, and I are skating. Three boys race by and one grabs PJ's hat. They play keep away. PJ is a good sport about it, until the biggest kid throws her hat up a tree. It snags on a branch beyond her reach. He skates away laughing.

I cut him off so fast he reels back and falls on his butt, collecting all the ice powder as he slides. Leaning over him, I ask him to please get PJ's hat out of the tree and give it back to her. I straighten up.

Bam! An ice ball hits my face. His friends have stockpiled a small mountain of them at the edge of the pond.

Powder Boy gets up and kicks me in the shin with the toe pick of his skate. The blade cuts through my pants, rips my skin. I lie on the ice, holding my leg, bombarded by clumps of ice and snow.

PJ is gone.

After what seems like hours, I see Killian running down the hill—no coat, no hat, no shoes—and PJ twenty yards behind him. I watch Killian slide all over the ice in his white athletic socks until he catches one, then another, and finally the third boy. He beats the living crap right out of them, then marches them over to the tree. "Take off your skates," he says to the biggest kid, "and climb up there." Powder Boy is crying and choke-coughing on his own fear, but he knocks the hat down and climbs out of the tree.

"Give it back to her and apologize like you mean it," Killian says.

They're so scared they're shaking in their jeans. PJ takes the stocking cap and puts it back on. Then Killian makes all three of them get down on their knees. They apologize to me a hundred million times.

"Now beat it," Killian says. He picks me up. Carries me home. PJ walks alongside us, sucking her thumb.

I got eight stitches in my shin that day. But right then I didn't care. I was safe in Killian's arms. Even with my cut-up leg.

Abraham

"Long-legged varmint." That's what they called Lincoln. He was my term project in Sister Imelda's class. And even though I never got to finish the paper, I have all the books here with me in the hospital. Lined up on the night table by my bed, Lincoln and the prairie years, and his life as a young lawyer, and Anne Rutledge (his first true love). Much later, his hardships as president. There're even books on the myths surrounding Lincoln. Like with martyred saints, miraculous words and deeds that got attri-buted to him. Sometimes it's hard to sort out fact from fiction.

I look around the hospital room. A dresser by the door full of stupid flowers. A chair in the corner. Another by the bed. And a night table with all these books. They belong to the St. Catherine's school library. Abe probably would have walked however many miles it took to return them, but me—how am I going to get there? I hope St. Catherine's rots in hell.

And I'm not giving back the books.

St. Catherine's

/ could tell you all about St. Catherine's—how I got expelled—but it's really stupid. No one around that place operates on more than two watts. And one of them is borrowed.

St. Cats. A school for rich girls. And me. A banker's kid on a sports scholarship. I hated it. Girls walking around with their noses turned up so high, they'd drown for sure if it rained. But that didn't stop the Banker from sending me. Didn't stop him from yanking me like a good tooth, roots and all. Right out of my life. A coin toss: Which do I hate more, him or St. Cats?

St. Cats lands facedown.

My dad, a loan officer here in Springfield, comes from a long line of Illinois bankers. Five, to be exact. All of them sniffing after other people's money. Our family's fifteen minutes of fame came in 1846 when

11

Cyrus Von Hartmann, my great-great et cetera, got together with some other Whigs and raised two hundred dollars to help pay the campaign expenses of a man running for Congress. A man so tall his trousers were forever creeping up past his ankles. And catch this: that lanky critter paid back every bit of the money except for seventy-five cents, shocking one and all.

Georgy

*G*eorgy was full of surprises, too. Didn't fit into any particular category. She wore wild-looking pants—bold colors and designs—with elastic around the ankles. Baggy sweatshirts, and men's T-shirts, dyed in bright greens and blues. The same rich colors of her tattoo. Until I met her, tattoos were something for Hells Angels, convicts, and other low-class amoebas.

She'd already dropped out of school for a year. Who knew why. And who knew what was in her duffel bags the day she lugged them down the hall of St. Catherine's. Heavy bags, too heavy for clothing. You could tell from the way they sagged over her shoulders. I watched from the hallway as Georgy dragged them into her bedroom, then kicked the door shut with her foot. After a few minutes of quiet. furious pounding began, like she was building a whole other room, and determined to do it in record time.

I stood outside Georgy's door, my fingers in my ears, imagining volcanic craters forming on the wall. I didn't want her to get into trouble, but something kept me from knocking. When the hammering stopped, the door slapped open to a new amazing world. The side wall was a Crayola explosion of colored rope: blue-and-yellow striped, speckled purple and orange, black-and-green diamondback. Yards and yards of nylon rope, all lengths and thicknesses, were hanging in a crazy pattern. There were brightly colored belts and slings, too. And a red helmet. Easy enough to figure that out, but I wondered about all the metal gizmos, hooks, wires, and serious-looking sprocket doodads.

Above her bed was a poster of a climber on a glacial peak. Thin clouds drifting by the bluest of aqua-blue skies. The fine print in the corner said "Mont Blanc."

I'd never seen anyone so enthusiastic about rocks in all my life. Climbers in Colorado name rocks the way people here name streets. There's Joshua Tree in her hometown, she told me. Red Rocks in Las Vegas. She can go on about the granite walls in Yosemite. Or the sandstone in Utah. On her bulletin board is a whole list of places in Europe she intends to climb someday.

If you listened, though, you could hear more

than excitement in her voice. There was sadness too. Pure homesick for rocks. That's what she was. No hills in Illinois. Unless you count the Indian burial mounds in Cahokia.

I couldn't imagine being shipped off to a place where I couldn't run. Adak, Alaska, for example. The sorry twist now is that there's land all around and not a race to run in. Except maybe the Special Olympics. Geek show for cripples like me.

Janey

Janey doesn't bring up the subject of St. Cats much. Maybe she knows. Janey is my evening nurse. She used to be Killian's girlfriend before Vietnam swallowed him alive. I always hoped they would get married but she's married to Someone Else now. Going to have Someone Else's baby.

When Janey finishes her rounds, she comes into my room.

"How about a game of Scrabble, Meghan?" We play that a lot or sometimes just talk until the midnight shift takes the floor. That's the best time here. The worst time is when anybody touches or looks at my leg. Or what was my leg. It's the absence of anything that keeps me from looking. They chopped it off below the knee.

"Listen." Janey picks up the box of letters and shakes it. She smiles. You'd think it was gold between her hands instead of a cardboard box with little wood blocks inside.

"No words in me today," I say. I roll on my side, away from her, but not really wanting her to leave. Can't stop thinking about it. Bloody stump. Missing leg. Right after they chop it off, they put on a fake one. No time to pay your respects to the dead and dearly departed. Right there on the slab table before you're even awake. Like they could fool you into thinking it's no big deal. In my mind, I imagine each step of the procedure, just like they told me, only in Technicolor. A bunch of gauze wrapped around the bloody end, then a bright white stump sock, then straps buried in layers of plaster, straps hooked to a belt around your waist to keep the cast from slipping down; no wrinkles around the ankles from these nylons. Finally, the prosthesis. Marionette-like straps hang from the thigh, and like magic, the thing just rides there, holding on to the stump by suction and pressure when you walk on it. If you do.

The day after Doctors Take More and Take Less put their saws away, they dragged me out of bed and made me stand up. And I called them every dirty word they deserved. Even in a drug haze, I remembered my toes tingling. Then I looked down and saw a rubber foot. What a sick, sick joke.

Janey sits down in the chair by my bed. "Maybe we could just talk, then, if you like," she says. "Or not talk."

Janey is the best nurse. For a while there was a suction tube in my leg by the knee, but they took it out. During that time I wouldn't let anyone near me except Janey. Couldn't bear to let anyone else see how bad it hurt. She's okay, because she doesn't make a big production of anything. Not like the weekend nurse, that redheaded sadist. I used to hold my pee all day rather than use a bedpan in front of her.

"I've been so hungry for olives lately," Janey says. "Last week it was Popsicles. A whole carton of them in four days."

I roll over and face her. "What kind of olives?"

"The big green Greek ones."

Suddenly I remember a dinner at our house a long time ago. Janey and Killian laughing at PJ because she had a black olive stuck on every fingertip. I look at Janey, wondering if she's thinking about that night too, knowing that she's not.

"I get that way about chocolate sometimes." I'm trying to find something to say, not wanting to think about her cravings and Someone Else's baby. Not wanting to think about now.

"I see you got some more flowers," she says.

Uh huh. Flowers from Old Lady Unser, who spent hours lurking behind her rosebushes just to yell at us if we stepped on her lawn.

"Take them to that little girl at the other end of the hall. The tonsillectomy."

"Oh, Meghan, are you sure? Don't you want them?"

"It looks like a damn funeral parlor in here," I say. "Besides, they're stinking up the place." Flowers and visitors. They can just drop dead.

"Do you need anything before I leave?" she asks.

"Killian." I didn't mean to say that but it just slipped out.

"Oh, Meghan."

I hear Janey's own hurt in those words and think of the time I climbed the oak when I was ten and watched her and Killian make out. Bit my finger to keep from laughing. Janey was snickering too, because Killian was sniffing around her ears. He had this thing for Janey's ears and he was snuffling and nibbling on them and I swear I almost dropped out of the tree like a crazed squirrel.

The next day I got Killian's goat but good. At the breakfast table I nuzzled his ears and ran. He chased me out the back door, through the lilac bushes that bordered our backyard, over two cyclone fences, and down a cinder alley where cats were pawing at the metal lids of garbage cans.

My morning run was off to a fast start.

I wish he'd come.

Corn

I've run in plenty of bean fields too, but it's nothing like corn. In the early summer the beans start to get all bushlike and then shrivel and look tired if rain doesn't come. But corn just sounds papery in the wind, setting off a chatter as if asking for water.

Corn was Lincoln's imagined audience, just like mine. Before his first speech—made in front of a Decatur drugstore—he'd only practiced on corn. Rows and rows and rows of corn. And they were all ears. Ha!

He knew all about corn. Helped his family clear fifteen acres in Macon County, where he did the planting. Tore up his hands from hoeing the rows. Some days he'd shuck corn from dawn to dusk. And when he ruined a book he'd borrowed from a neighbor, he worked three days pulling fodder to pay for it. Every stalk was bare when he finished. Not a single ear.

Like him I was barefoot in the cornfields until a couple of years ago. I hired onto a DeKalb crew, detasseling. Six-thirty A.M. you'd begin and work until sunset. Stalks were head high and heat stayed trapped in the rows. If an early-morning rain came, there'd be steam by noon and your clothes would be wetter than a baby's diaper, full of sweat and salt, which burned into the long leaf cuts on your legs.

Crew bosses would stand on truck beds and watch the black girls race through the half-mile rows. The girls would be sitting in a group, rested and cheerful, by the time I finished. Then came the order no more sitting or you'd be fired. They claimed the blacks never pulled the tassels, that they just moseyed through the rows, and that was why. But for $1.40 an hour, I began to think they knew something I didn't.

After the corn had been detasseled, a fine yellow dust settled all over you—feet, neck, and back. There was one night when it was suddenly torture to bathe. Raw sores broke out on my back from the pollen and the DDT. And it was three days before I could walk without feeling like I'd fallen asleep with my feet in a red-ant pile. I never entered the fields barefoot after that, and never past July, when it was knee-high. But I'd stop by sometimes in the late afternoons because it was still beautiful to watch the slow dance of corn in the breeze.

The Vanity of Feet

eet are funny things. So is vanity. But I never would have thought of them as related; that is, before the nuns. The nuns talked a lot about vanity when I was in grammar school, especially to the girls. Although when I think about it, most of the examples were men: Samson and his long hair; the rich merchants in the New Testament with their fine silks and robes. How it got to be a girl thing, I'll never know.

I was never vain about my hair. It's brown—the brown color of good soil—and touches my shoulders straight all around. It's thick, but not unique or special. My face has a well-scrubbed German look. My eyes are a pale Irish gray. The rest of me is lanky and I feel like clothes never quite fit me right. The one thing I really liked about myself was my feet. Since they were covered up most of the time, I figured that didn't hurt me in the vanity department.

I liked the high arches and the way my toes gradually got smaller in a smooth little row. Not like some people whose toes stick up every which way and are full of bunions and corns and a million other ugly bumps.

And I liked that the nails all had half-moons. When I would stretch out on my bed, I'd look down and see all those little white moons lined up like dancers waiting for a matching partner.

Sam

For a while here in the hospital, I was on one of the adult floors. Had this old woman for a roommate who cried nonstop. When she slept she snored like a 747 getting ready for takeoff. No joke. It was so loud, none of the aides bothered checking her on night rounds. It drove me crazy for two days. Then I threw a stainless steel water pitcher through the television screen.

Sam got me transferred out of there PDQ. Sam Levin is a nut cracker. Not your typical shrink, according to Janey. She's very fond of him. Personally, I think the cheese fell off his cracker a long time ago. And I haven't decided whether or not to add him to my list: Doctor Nut Cracker.

So far, Sam's got a couple of things in his favor. He's Jewish, so no Holy Mary Mother of God and Jesus stuff. The other thing—he never pokes around at my stump like the rest of them, although he can get pretty nosy about other issues. My family, for instance. I guess he's worried the Banker and I are going to knock each other off. Not the bang bang shotgun quickie type of murder but the slow-drip method spread out over days of not talking. Until one of us steps on a minefield and there's a nasty explosion of words that blows the silence to hell. Maybe we will kill each other. If I live long enough.

Blazes

We're halfway through another thrilling session when Sam leans forward and says, "So, Meghan. Had any dreams lately?"

"Maybe." I look away from him and think about lying. I lie to Sam a lot. Not the kind of lying where you make things up, but the kind where you leave things out.

"I'd like to hear," he says. "And no censoring, please."

Censoring. That's Sam's word. But hey, why bother with euphemisms? A sin of omission is just a big fat lie. "Nothing unusual. Just more charbroiled babies."

He flips the page of his spiral notebook and says, "I'm interested."

"At seventy dollars an hour," I say, "you'd find dog turds downright fascinating."

He ignores my comment.

What the hell. As long as I'm here anyway. From my window I see a winter crow in the distance. It fades into a tiny black speck, but I keep staring anyway. "I'm standing in this room. It's pretty dark except there's this weird kind of orange glow coming from somewhere. All around me are babies and young children. All sleeping and lined up on tiny cots. I'm just kind of wandering up and down between the rows of beds. All of a sudden the light shifts and gets really bright underneath me. I look down . . ."

"Go on," says Sam.

"It's flames. They're covering the floor." In spite of myself, I realize I've wrapped my arms around myself. Sam doesn't seem to notice. I let my hands drop to my lap and go on. "The flames move slow at first. Then catch the edges of the blankets that are hanging over the cots. Soon each little kid is surrounded in a circle of fire. I pick up a baby and try to run out the door. But I can't."

"Why not?"

"Hell, I don't know. I just can't. I get as far as the doorway. I can feel my foot rocking on the sill, but I just can't step past it. That's when I look up and see a man, standing off by himself in the yard. I yell at him to help. All those babies will burn. I'm not really saying the words; it's more like I'm talking with my eyes only he won't look. He's busy poking through his wallet. Then he has a huge wad of bills in his hand and the wallet disappears. When I beg he looks up and drops the cash. Finally, I think, he's going to help. But he takes a comb out of his pocket instead and plays it like a harmonica. I can even see him tapping his foot, like he's keeping time to the music."

"And then?" Doctor Nut Cracker doesn't bother to look up from his notepad.

"Somehow—I don't know how—I'm outside with a baby. I put it down on the ground and go back for another. Then Killian comes running out with a kid and sets it down next to the first." I stop to catch my breath. Sam's pen is still scratching across the page fast and furious like a striking match in the rain.

"What then?" he finally asks.

"That's all."

"That's it?"

"Yup."

Sam raises an eyebrow at me.

I stare back at him. I've told him enough for one day.

He stretches, clicks the pen shut, and slips it into his shirt pocket. "What about the man? Know who he was?"

I shrug, seeing Killian racing back toward the fire, with me swearing at him, begging him not to go, telling him that it's too late. But he doesn't stop. Suddenly the man is blocking the door, and for a minute I think Killian will have to stop, because that man won't let him in. But the man vanishes slowly, becoming a paler version of himself just like in *Star Trek* when someone is being transported to another universe. When he disappears completely, Killian goes back into the fire.

And I stand there as the flames explode, and glass shatters, feeling the heat eat at my face.

"Did the man remind you of anyone?" Sam asks again.

I yawn. How stupid does he think I am?

PJ and Her Abacus

*T*here're a lot of little kids on this floor, but I don't mind. They remind me of my sister Penelope Jean. PJ. She's in the sixth grade. Normal in everything but math. In the afternoons she takes calculus at the public high school. They call her the banker's brat, say she'll be just like my dad, foreclosing on all the farmers. But she's tough. Just goes about her business.

Her thing for numbers started when she was about five. She had just gotten this new abacus from the dime store. She had seen it in the school supply aisle at Woolworth's and that's all she could talk about for a week until my mom finally went back and bought it for her. She slept with it at nap time, one thumb in her mouth and the other quietly rattling those little beads.

By August she could multiply and divide on it.

Tell you things you never thought about or cared to know. How many chocolate chips are in a one-pound bag. The number of ceramic tiles in the bathroom.

That summer I had a little red transistor radio that fit real snug in my back pocket when PJ and I would pedal our bikes out to Grass Lake. I'd connect my cane pole and sit there staring at the red-and-white bobber rocking on the water, my mind empty. One day when I was fishing for bluegills, catching little bitsy ones and letting them go, the radio gave a static gasp and went dead. I picked it up and shook it. PJ, sitting on the bank next to me, kept fiddling with her beads in a dreamy way. Suddenly there was Walter Cronkite's voice giving the latest war casualties. PJ began to add them. After that, that's what she did. Every day. Every time she heard the noonday news.

It gave me the jitters. I wanted her to go back to counting chocolate chips.

Meanings

*I*f you look in a good dictionary, you can find over a hundred definitions for running. For example: 1) Lincoln ran for office in 1832 and lost. 2) If you eat green corn you'll get the runs. 3) In 1967 a drunk driver ran into my mother.

The next day she was gone. Like my leg.

That night, about ten o'clock, the sheriff came to our door. I saw him from my bedroom window walking slow, like he was looking where to put his feet. First I thought Killian had collected one too many parking tickets because he'd just gotten his license and could never remember to feed the meters. But there was something grim about the way he carried himself down the walk to our door. And I knew even before he rang the bell, something terrible had happened. I flew down the stairs two and three at a time and the sound of the doorbell kept ringing inside of me and wouldn't stop. I opened the door. The sheriff already had his hat in one hand, turning it slowly by the brim with the other. First, he looked at me, then behind me, up at my dad.

"Julius," he said, "there's been a terrible accident."

I could hear Killian thumping down the stairs. The three of us stood there staring at the sheriff, waiting for words we didn't want to hear. I remember the Banker's breathing, raspy like he'd just run the half mile. Warm irregular puffs grazed the back of my head.

We got to the emergency room pronto—PJ still sleepy in her pajamas—but she was in a coma. When Father Kelso came I was sitting in the hall by her door. I jumped up, told him he couldn't go in, but my dad and Killian came out, my dad said he'd asked him to come, and Killian held me away from the door, his arms tight around me. I shouted at him to stop when he anointed her feet. "She's not that bad off," I yelled. But she died that night without ever regaining consciousness.

At the funeral Mrs. Clements kept crying and wringing her hands. I knew she felt like it was partly her fault, because my mom had gone out of her way to take her home after their monthly game of canasta. She had just gotten back on the highway when she was hit. I wanted to tell Mrs. Clements that it was all right, that it wasn't her fault, but I just couldn't find it in me to say so.

In his sermon, Father Kelso said we must find it in our hearts to forgive. I sat there and chewed on my lips until I could taste the blood, I was so mad.

I kick and stomp and rage like a bull, because I fight and never forgive anybody anything.

I think I must be a terrible person inside.

Running

*B*efore I could walk, I could run. Put one foot in front of the other and kept going. Sometimes I'd forget things at the corner store just so I'd have to run back. When my out-of-town uncle left his hat, I chased his car for two blocks. Caught him and got a dollar.

In September, when I was back to school, I'd already be dreaming about endless summers of running. I'd picture myself running when the snow was too high or the storm runoff too swift. I'd wait for the charged air of March to come and go. For the sheets of water covering the fields to shrink and disappear into the soil. Then I could believe I'd be in the cornfields soon—running faster than summer lightning.

It's short sprints I love the most.

Bang! Off like a bullet, cutting a straight path. A

hundred yards. I don't think about it. I just do it. Wind pushes against my legs, my chest, my arms, and I push back.

Out of the corner of my eye I see my competitors. They are eager, determined, strong. So am I. Eat my dust. I push harder until there's nothing in my vision but the line of victory. And I lean into it. Running is the thing.

Running was what I did best.

Socks

Sam pulls a chair up next to my bed. He sits down and crosses his legs and I am forced to look at his stupid feet.

"What do you want to talk about today, Meghan?"

"Your socks." He's wearing one blue and one gray one. Neither matches his green tweed suit. What a fashion plate I've lucked into. He's color-blind. Or better, he just doesn't care.

"You like them?"

"No." I cross my arms and look at the ceiling. I never used to wear socks. Only during bone cold winter days and when I was running. Now I'd do just about anything to be able to pull them up over two feet.

"Well then, maybe we shouldn't waste time on them. Maybe we should talk about you."

That's the last damn thing I want to talk about right now. "Do you know that when Congressman Lincoln was in Washington, his wife ran him all over Capitol Hill looking for a pair of plaid stockings for Eddie, their little boy?"

He nods and looks down. I think the genius just figured out his socks are two different colors.

I try to imagine the Banker coming home with a pair of socks for me—the cotton extra thick in the heels for breaking in a pair of running shoes. But it's too late for that. And sure too late for Eddie, who hardly got to wear those tartan stockings anyway. He died when he was only four. I wonder if he had them on when they buried him. How can you not love a man who shopped for his kids at a time when most men wouldn't be caught dead going into a store?

"How about your dad, Meghan?"

"You're about as subtle as an elephant in the bathroom," I say.

"Hmmm." That's all he says. Then he just sits there, looking at me with a dopey half-smile on his face.

I hate those stupid pauses. Pushing me to talk. I almost always give in. "When I was a kid there was this boy in the neighborhood named Donnie who lost a good chunk of his index finger to a lawn mower. He could take the stub and rest it inside his nose, making it look like his finger was so far up there you could practically see him scratching his brain."

Sam laughs.

"Donnie was my first true love." I put a hand over my heart. "He bought me a fifty-nine-cent box of butter mints. I was pretty sure we would be married one day. But to think of it now, it's not that funny of a trick and I don't think I'll ever get married."

"Why not, Meghan?"

"Would you buy a bicycle with one wheel?"

The Boot

You should have seen the Banker's face that night I got booted out of St. Cats. There we were, the four of us—the dean of students, the housing director, Georgy, and me—cozy peas in a pod waiting for the Banker to arrive. Georgy's mom was too far away to make it the same day. Poor Georgy would have to relive the whole sorry scene.

In walks the Banker, his face serious as a Russian in a spy movie. Sitting at her big wood desk to greet him was the dean, Sister Pauline, who wasn't too bad as nuns go. But behind her stood the housing director, Sister Adele, whom I'm about as fond of as cancer. Above both of them was a gold cross that hung on the wall. It was like a scene from a B movie, the cross and all, like the director was trying to show you that God was on their side, while off to the corner on a narrow couch sat Georgy and me.

The Banker removed his coat and scarf and folded them over the back of a chair. Then he turned his chair catty-cornered to both sides of the ring and sat down. He alternated between watching and listening to the good sisters in the cross corner and staring at the evil perpetrators in the other.

He listened and his face grew redder. He stared at the bandage plastered on Sister Adele's nose, then shot me a look of hate.

I thought about shrugging my shoulders.

When they were finished with the whole sorry story, all he said to me was, "Pack your bags, young lady."

I think that kind of disappointed the nuns. They were waiting for him to tell me how bad, foolish, ungrateful, and disrespectful I was. He saved that conversation for the car ride home. When we pulled into the driveway, I opened the back of the station wagon to unload my gear, but the Banker said, "Just leave it and go to your room." I thought then he was so mad he was afraid he was going to hit me. But now I think it was something more than that. Something he didn't want me to see. Tears of disappointment on top of rage.

I spent the next two days in my room.

Drafted

*I*t's odd that we do things we never would have imagined ourselves doing. Like Killian—a pacifist—going to Vietnam. His great love was poetry: Keats, Byron, Wordsworth, that crew. Dylan Thomas, too. He grew his hair long and would stand in front of the mirror with a face full of fluffy shaving cream and say things like, "I wandered lonely as a cloud."

Killian's world was one of pretty words, strung together with fine cornsilk. If there hadn't been a war, he would have gone on to the University of Illinois and studied his poets and married Janey and taken a job in a small college town and lived happily et cetera after, but Killian got served a bowl of sour cherries, pits and all. He was drafted in 1968, when he was nineteen years old.

Not long after he got the news, we were sitting glumly in my bedroom hardly saying a word to each other. Killian was at my desk staring at the picture of Lincoln taped on the wall above my lamp. He traced the beard with his finger. "I bet Lincoln would have had a thing or two to say about the Vietnam war." President Polk shouldn't have started the war with Mexico, young Abe had said, and he talked of a people's revolution, the right to rise up when they feel that the government is in the wrong.

But in '68 it seemed like the more people took to the streets to protest the war, the more troops they sent overseas. And when they murdered Robert Kennedy and Martin Luther King, Jr., I thought the whole world had gone to hell. But what I remember most clearly about that year is the day Killian left and PJ stood there with her abacus crying good-bye. "Thirty thousand, Killian," she said. "Thirty thousand."

To Burn or Not to Burn

*P*acifist in Vietnam. Not hard to figure if you know our family. Killian almost burnt his draft card the afternoon it came in the mail. Janey said no. They ought to make a ceremony of it. Go up to Chicago for a burning. Abbie Hoffman and a bunch of Yippies were going to be there. A big bonfire was planned.

Fireworks exploded when the Banker found out. Shouting. Doors slamming. He called Killian a good-for-nothing. Unpatriotic. Had Killian by the collar, danced him around the room like a rag doll. In between sobs Killian kept mumbling, "No killing, I can't," his voice all cloudy with snot. He was crying and holding on to my dad and trying to make him understand.

"I've raised a pansy for a son," the Banker yelled, his face all red. Then he shoved Killian aside and walked out the door, slamming it behind him.

Killian didn't come out of his room all that night. By the next morning, he had changed his mind. It wasn't that he didn't feel strongly about the war— just eager to please, pacify. That's all. Killian would cut his own nose off just to please someone else. He couldn't take being at odds with the Banker anymore. He was already a disappointment. Choosing poetry over banking.

I'll never forgive the Banker for talking Killian out of burning his draft card. If he could have seen Killian take on those three bullies at the ice pond, he never would have called him a coward. Killian could have burnt his draft card quietly and slipped over the border to Canada. Not exactly a Hollywood ending, but I don't trust those anyway.

Our House Is a
Very Fine House

*T*he place where we once all lived happily together has two stories and a brick porch. A strange gothic-looking turret shoots up on the side of the house. It's made of brick. Grandfather Hartman built it in 1926. Right after losing a big poker game. Lived in there until he died. The Banker wanted to tear it down, but my mom talked him out of it. They were going to be married soon, and Catholic families grew pretty fast in those days. They kept the tower, turned it into the Banker's office. It's become sort of a landmark around Springfield. Folks call it the city silo.

The rest of the house is more traditional. Bedrooms upstairs. High ceilings with plaster molding of leaves and vines.

My bedroom is big and kind of empty because I like open spaces. PJ has a lot of junk in her room but hides it under the bed each time she cleans. At the end of the hall is Killian's bedroom. No one has touched his room since he left for Vietnam.

At the other end of the hall is the largest bedroom of all, my dad's. He hasn't changed a thing since my mom died. Double bed. Plain white chenille spread. A crucifix hangs on the wall above it. Behind the crucifix are two dried palm strands. The night table on my mom's side has a Bible and a Hummel figurine. A little boy fishing. The pole has been broken and reglued. Newspapers and pocket change cover the other table. And in the corner by the window is an Ethan Allen rocking chair that the Banker bought for her when Killian was a baby.

Downstairs, the foyer is full of dark oak paneling. On one wall hangs a row of blue china plates. On the other wall are paintings of stodgy-looking Hartmans in dark suits. It's enough to make you take up darts. Killian used to say it was the House of Usher. Get out while you can.

The living-room floors are covered with big rugs from Iran that are old and dusty-smelling. A shiny brown shows through the mahogany-stained arms of the chairs. They're upholstered with tufted backs and ugly as hell. Stuck in the corner behind the potted ferns is an upright piano from the twenties. No one plays it anymore and it's way out of key. But the old leather couch is nice. Even though I know he never did, I imagine Lincoln sitting there, winding that old watch of his with a brass key.

The kitchen is my favorite part of the house. It's sunny and has been remodeled. There's a giant ashtray on the kitchen table that PJ made in summer camp. Before my mom died, I always used to do my homework at that table even though I had a desk in my room. The smells and sounds of dinner being prepared helped me concentrate. But now when our housekeeper, Mrs. Blanch, cooks, it doesn't smell the same.

Off of the kitchen is a small dining room with a picture wall full of us from the time we were babies. There's one when I'm just a few minutes old—fat face, no hair, blowing spit bubbles, looking like a moron. Another of PJ's First Communion. Killian on the banana seat of his new bike, leaning over the high handlebars.

On the sideboard are a million more of those dust-catching knickknacks my mom collected when she worked at a Hallmark store. Stocking cards for all occasions. Selling gift wrap and Russell Stover candies. Unwrapping cratefuls of Holly Hobbie figurines. And Charles Schultz's Peanuts gang.

Sometimes I look at those little figurines sitting there all sad and dusty and wonder if they miss her.

Pop Kelley's Teeth

When my mom's dad died, a long time before she did, I thought he went to a place called Heaven's Tavern, where they served beer and cotton candy. I was old enough to miss him and to understand that he left all his good stuff behind. I asked for two things of his. One I got, the other I didn't, and the cigar box I just took. It has three singing Dutchmen on the inside lid and smells a little bit of tobacco if I hold it close and sniff the corner.

Pop Kelley told the best stories about this hobo named Johnny, who would hop trains and ride clear across the United States. The adventures of Johnny the Tramp. That's what he called the stories. Johnny always got into tight spots but would manage to escape just in time. The story would always end the same way—Johnny getting this great breakfast of bacon, scrambled eggs, and fried green tomatoes.

The tomatoes were always cooked just right in the bacon grease. Not too much salt or pepper.

Most of the time Pops would tell these stories in the early evening before the living-room lamps were turned on. The fading light seemed to be right inside me along with the jazzy sadness of crickets, and it was only the orange glow of his Dutch Masters that kept me from feeling all strange and peppery.

He'd take these long puffs right at the really important parts of the story and I'd watch the bright tip of his cigar intensify just like my being afraid for Johnny. I hoped, I prayed, I fidgeted in my seat, waiting for Johnny to escape the tight spot he was wedged into.

It was at these moments that I most especially remember the smells of smoke and beer. Pops always drank. Stroh's in the afternoons. The smoky smell of his cigar was like a campfire, heavy in the air. Behind that was a milder scent of tobacco, a freshly cut meadow. I pictured Johnny running through some wheat field trying to catch a passing train. A pack of wild dogs would be chasing him, their teeth glinting in the golden sunset, the fur on their necks standing tall like shafts of wheat. But Johnny would keep running faster, his eye on the billowing smokestack of the train as it chugged along. Cartoon melodrama. And I loved it.

Johnny always survived, like I said, but Pops didn't. He got sick and lapsed into a coma. Then a brain aneurism finished him off. They said his liver was green and shriveled when they cut him open. It rained the day we buried him and I got hives underneath my arms.

After the funeral Grammy asked me what I wanted. I named the two things, the first was one of his hand-kerchiefs. Pops would never use tissues. He always carried a wadded-up hankie in his back pocket. More than once he'd spit into his palm and dab his hankie in there before wiping dirt off my face.

Grammy tried to give me a new-in-the-box hand-kerchief, but I wouldn't take it. She'd thrown the old ones away. I ran to the trash can, dug through the coffee grounds and cigarette butts. I tried to keep my tears from spattering on the damp news-paper. Tried to keep anyone from seeing how des-perate I was. Desperate for an old stained hankie. Gone. Already carted away. It made me love her less and long for him all the more. But because of the hankie, she couldn't deny me the teeth.

Pops had pulled two of his back molars with needle-nose pliers and left them on his dresser. I took them and put them in the cigar box. On the six-hour drive back to Springfield I sat with the box on my lap and shook it every now and then just to hear his bones talking.

I've put anything that was special to me inside that box. Like Killian's letters from Vietnam. A blue ribbon PJ won in a math contest. One of Georgy's carabiner rings. There's also a handful of photographs, including my favorite one of Lincoln.

Scrabble for Truth

"You really ought to finish that report on Lincoln and turn it in," says Janey. She draws out seven little tiles of wood and arranges them on her rack.

"Think so?" Maybe she doesn't know about me getting expelled after all. Which happened around the same time as my leg. A damn tornado of events.

"Definitely." She smiles, her face golden in the soft lamplight by my bed. Janey's good with words. Beats me most of the time we play Scrabble. That's one reason she and Killian got on so well. They both loved words. I could have pictured them in old age, fighting over the crossword puzzle in the Sunday paper.

"I'll think about it." Right. *Dear Dean, Enclosed is my long-awaited essay on Abraham Lincoln. Sincerely, Meghan Hartman (whom you recently expelled).* I draw my square chips and line them up.

It's Monday evening, Janey's first night back after the weekend. "So," she says, nonchalant-like, "has Killian come by yet to see you?"

"No." What lousy tiles. "Do you think he'll come?"

"He'll come," she tells me.

How can she be so sure? I rearrange the letters in front of me and try not to think about it. One vowel, not much to start off with. I like word games but I'm hampered because of my poor spelling. For example, is it *gnu* or *gnyu*? Janey lets me look in the dictionary but I try not to abuse the privilege.

She goes for the six or seven-letter words like *pogrom* and *enclave*. I go for the smaller ones. Sometimes I add an *s* to her words and get a fair amount of points, which is nice.

Janey lays first: *ataxia*.

"Good one."

"*X* is always a challenge." She draws more letters.

We play by our own rules. Some nights we allow abbreviations or acronyms just to keep it interesting. If I get in a jam I can use a nasty four-letter word, but that doesn't happen too often. Tonight is different. I get lucky with six letters, intersect one of her vowels, and use the nastiest word I can think of: *FAMILY*.

That's another horrible thought I have. Maybe we never were a "once upon a time" happy family. Maybe I just thought it. Because that's what I was told. The way someone tells you there's a tooth fairy and a Santa Claus and an Easter bunny. But soon enough you're wise to all that. How stupid you feel then.

I bet when you turn eighteen they tell you there is no God. That's what happened to Killian the dreamer. Something shattered his world and tore out a piece of him.

"Oh, Janey." I feel the heavy weight of things in my head. How to stop thinking? "I wish we could play Scrabble all night long."

Just a Bruise

I have terrible thoughts that plague me. One is that pieces of me will keep rotting off and soon I'll be nothing. And what is nothing? If you're nothing do you know it? Or do you not even know that you're nothing? Are you dirt that can't think? And what if there is a genuine afterlife and it's worse than this one? Like the sailor surrounded by water he can't drink. Or that man in mythology who gets his insides eaten out every day and wakes up the next day to have it happen all over again. And if there is a God—let's face it, I don't see very many signs that she cares about what's going on around here. Like the war, and all the charming crap she's dropped at my doorstep lately.

I can't tell Sam this. Every time I try, it gets stuck in my throat. I about choke on it. I swallow it back down and it rattles around in my ribs and finally settles. And at night I still lie awake. I thought I'd sleep a little better now that I have my own room. No more crying woman. No more crying. No.

My leg still hurts so bad in ways that don't make sense. My foot stings and itches even though it's gone. Not at the end of the stump where all the nerve endings are but down where my foot used to be. It's like the space where my leg once was remembers. And has its own pain.

It's odd, because at first there was no pain. There was some soreness that would come and go, nothing that seemed unusual. I was used to one kind of little running pain or another; it's part of the athlete's package. But then a bruise showed up on my calf. On the outside, below the knee. I didn't think much of it, because I'd banged a weight against it in the gym. When it didn't go away or do its fading rainbow routine, I knew something was wrong. Wrong as cancer can be. So fast and final I'm still out of breath.

How could something so bad come so quietly? But I knew. The doctor sitting behind his desk made me think of the silent sheriff who came to our door. When I think back on that day I'm not sure what I thought or believed myself.

I had just gotten the boot from St. Cats. I was home. Grounded. In my room for two days. I sat on my bed with a deck of plastic-coated cards, flipping one at a time into a hat. When the deck ran out, I'd pick them up and start all over. On one of those pick-up rounds, I felt a sharp twinge in my leg. Did I really know something was wrong then, or was I just look-ing for an excuse to get out? I guess I knew.

I think the Banker knew too when I showed it to him. He was in his study silo reading the evening paper. I knocked on the door. From the ankle, I pulled up the right leg of my sweatpants and showed him the bruise.

Nine o'clock the next morning I was smelling isopropyl alcohol, the perfume of choice in all doc-tors' waiting rooms. I had counted all the magazines and was contemplating how the receptionist could make that beehive hairdo of hers stand up so straight without a bottle of Elmer's.

My heart thump-thumped when they called my name. I think the Banker was nervous too. He'd been on the same magazine page since he sat down. I stood up to follow the nurse and saw that he'd been staring at an ad for Newport cigarettes.

The nurse patted the crinkly white paper on the exam table, a sign for me to sit my butt right down. She took my vital signs and left, closing the door quietly behind her. Then came the doctor, who poked and prodded and asked me a million questions. Like it was all routine, the nurse came in again and took my blood. They did some stat tests with it. By two o'clock that afternoon, I was checked into the hospi-tal. X ray. Biopsy. Then those two clowns Take More and Take Less.

Now my leg is history.

Where Is It?

I tried to find out what they did with my sawed-off leg. No one around this chop shop seems to know. Anyone who does, plays ignorant. Lots of people get separated from their body parts, according to Sam. Parts of Einstein's brain are in Ohio. A museum in Italy has Galileo's finger under glass. And Saint Catherine of Siena (the one they named St. Cats after) has her head in one church, her body in another. But they're dead. And I'm not. Not yet anyway. And I want to know where my goddamn leg is.

That's exactly what I ask Doctor Take Less. "Where is my leg?"

His face turns redder than cherry lip gloss. "Ah . . . er . . . " He flips open the chart and stares at it instead of at me. I think of PJ's tonsils in a jar of formaldehyde given to her by the doctor when she was six. She kept them on her dresser until they started to flake apart like those miniature water-filled snow bubbles.

"It went to the lab," he says. "We send all . . . er . . . samples to the lab."

"And then where did it go from there?" I heard that hospitals sell a woman's afterbirth. All those rich nutrients. Cold cream companies buy it. Maybe they threw my leg in as part of the bargain. Maybe not.

"I really don't know." He closes the chart and says he'll check in on me tomorrow.

Maybe in a hundred years they'll take my leg out of some freezer and stick it in a Smithsonian display case: *Cancer in the 1970s claimed thousands of lives a year. Leg courtesy of Meghan Hartman.*

Maybe Lincoln could figure out where it is. His mind was detective sharp. He came close to losing his own feet when he was young. In the blizzard of 1830 after four feet of snow had fallen. Freezing rain and more snow fell. The Lincoln family had it bad, hardly any corn or wood. Abe tried to get to a neighbor's house but the ice broke when he crossed the Sangamon River. His feet were so bad off by the time he got there that they had to be put in snow to take out the frostbite, then rubbed in grease. No grease could save my leg.

But I don't think that's what Sam wants to hear about. After Doctor Take Less leaves, Sam pulls up a chair. It's refreshing to see a doctor without a white coat. Sometimes it gets to looking like a blizzard in here.

We chitchat for the first couple of minutes. Not exactly about the weather but almost. It comes like a sudden storm when he says to me, "It must be hard going through all this without your mother."

Why doesn't he just punch me in the stomach? "What is this? Talk about Meghan's losses day?"

"You've been through some terrible things," he says.

I shrug and stare at the pile of books by my bed, like I'm reading the spines.

"Meghan?"

Finally I look at him. "Yeah," I mumble, "I guess so."

When Sam leaves, I lie back and close my eyes, listening to footsteps in the hallway. Even, symmetrical sounds. Soon I imagine I hear Killian's footsteps, but I know they're too loud to be his.

Boot Camp

Killian's first letters. I devoured them along with tea and cheese sandwiches when the afternoon mail arrived. They were always short. Sometimes only a paragraph or two. I could memorize them easy. Play them over and over in my head on early-evening runs.

The first night it rained. They marched them from one place to another. Soaking wet. Killian said they were part of a cattle line led down tiled hallways to be poked and inspected. Branded and shaved. They finally went to bed at 6:30.

I waited for his next letter, for him to tell me all about drills, push-ups, and bayonet training. But it was all about smells. The smell of powder and gun oil. Of tobacco smoked in hurried unison. Of boot polish, Brasso, and floor wax. Killian was doing his best not to be noticed, he said. That was the key to getting through without trouble. But you could tell he didn't like it one little bit. He never said so in the letters that came to us, not the ones the Banker would read. In those letters he said they made him buy U.S. Savings Bonds. He didn't object. It was something the Banker started us doing before we could walk. One guy in Killian's company refused. His life was hell for weeks.

The letters he wrote to Janey—those told you a whole different story. Sometimes she'd read parts of them directly to me. We hated his drill sergeant as much as he did. Subhuman and stupid. I remember he made them all drink a capful of Tide because someone left a dirty sock on the floor. And when another guy's sister died in a car crash, the drill sergeant still forced him to do an eight-hour march with the rest of the men. Right after he had gotten the news. That's the only time Killian caught hell, because he sassed back and said that wasn't right.

In Springfield, hardly anyone would oppose going to war. America right or wrong. It was your duty. Something you did whether you wanted to or not. Fight communism. Killian didn't buy all that jazz but he was too afraid of bringing shame on the family. Afraid of being called a coward. Afraid of being afraid.

Killian had started his freshman year at Illinois. He should have been safe, at least until he finished.

But the year before, President Johnson changed the selection order beginning with the nineteen-year-olds first. And college didn't seem to matter, not to our local draft board.

First Postcard

*I*t's 3:20 P.M. when PJ comes into my room. She's walked five blocks from school and her cheeks are red with cold. The smell of cold lingers in her duffle coat and scarf. Cold drifts from her pockets as she empties them: two PayDays, a Milky Way, a Zero candy bar. In the other pocket, a Suzy Q. I bite the cellophane with my teeth, tear it open. PJ takes her half and licks the cream on the side before biting into the chocolate cake.

"You bought a good stash today."

"I know." She doesn't talk very much. Keeps her most personal thoughts to herself just like Lincoln. I don't press. I pat the bed. "Have a seat, PJ." She was four before she talked. Slow as molasses in January, kids teased. But she just didn't want to be bothered.

"You mean it?" Surprised delight covers her face. It's the first time I've dropped my invisible force shield since the operation. She throws her scarf and coat in the chair.

"Of course I mean it. I've got all this extra legroom." I laugh but PJ doesn't. "Where's your sense of humor?"

"That's not funny, Meghan."

"It is funny. Just damn hilarious."

"You don't have to cuss, Meghan."

"I do goddamn too have to cuss. You have no sense of humor, PJ."

"I do too have humor. That's just not funny. When you really think it's funny I'll laugh."

"I just said I thought it was goddamn hilarious." PJ looks down. For a moment I think she's going to cry, but I know her better than that. "Listen, PJ, all funny things are sad. That's the truth."

PJ scratches behind her ear. "Let's split the Milky Way bar next."

"Sounds good to me."

PJ reaches for it and tears the crimped edge with her nimble fingers. I watch the ends of her hair skate across the smooth red of her cheeks. PJ used to wear a ponytail. Schoolboys pulled on it without mercy, so she cut it off. Now it's short and wavy—almost wiry, not at all like Killian's.

"How was school today?"

She pulls the chocolate bar away from her mouth. A thin strand of caramel drops down her chin. "I got a new Texas Instruments calculator. It's

65

got a zillion buttons, Meghan. Want to see it?"

"Sure." Long way from the stained-glass colors of an abacus.

She hops off the bed and goes to the chair. Beneath her coat is her book bag and she roots inside it. "Oh, I brought more letters, too," she says, "from your friend in Colorado." She puts three of them on the nightstand. "Aren't you ever going to write her back, Meghan? She writes you all the time. I get the letters from the mailbox when I get home, but Saturday Dad beat me to it and he kept that one."

"Are you sure?" I ask.

"Positive. It was blue. Just like all these."

I want to cry with rage or hurt. I don't know which. To think of him reading my mail. I swallow hard. "PJ, let's see that calculator."

She goes back and digs it out of the bag, holds it close to her face like she's myopic, but I know it's only because she's so excited. She keys in some numbers. I watch, reminded of all her brain can do. She climbs back on the bed and hands it to me. "Look."

She's playing calculator Scrabble: word combinations with numbers. It's a game she's been playing for years. Today's word is *shill.* She asks me if I know it. "Sure. It's half of a shillelagh, so it must mean a broken stick."

She giggles. "It's a swindler, silly."

"I knew that."

Then she laughs again and it hits me what a little

kid she still is. Except for her mind when it wraps itself around numbers.

They've come from Chicago to test her. And once some men in suits from Washington. Mixed in with her thing for numbers is what they call a creative component. When she was still a teeny thing, she'd make you cut her apple in half sideways so she could look at the star pattern. Twinkle twinkle little star.

I clear the small screen and punch in the numbers 5150. It reads "OSIS." I hand it back to PJ. Suddenly I'm afraid she'll slip away silently as morning fog through bare tree branches like everything else that I love.

"Osis?" She licks the chocolate off her thumb and studies it inquisitively instead of the word, as if an answer could be found in the skin's genetic hoops and swirls.

"You give? Hypnosis. Cirrhosis."

"Oh, a suffix. That's good."

"Shill was better. That's the word of the day."

She turns off the calculator and closes the plastic cover. "I got to go now, Meghan. Mrs. Blanch will be waiting for me."

"I know." Mrs. Blanch comes in the morning and stays until the pot roast is out of the oven.

"She's making date-nut bread today, my favorite."

I look down at the pile of wrapper trash and wonder if PJ's the one with a hollow leg.

"I could bring you some tomorrow."

"No. The dates stick in my teeth and then I'll have to floss. I hate to floss."

She puts on her coat, runs her fingers down the spiny stack of Lincoln books piled on my nightstand, before she slips her hands into mittens.

"You think he really sat on that old sofa in our living room, Meghan?"

"It's possible." I'm surprised and not surprised that PJ has thought of this. When I was a little kid I used to talk to him all the time.

"But not probable." She sounds grown-up and a little sad.

When she leaves I hide the evidence of our sugar party from the nurses. Wrapper and cellophane in my nightstand drawer. I take the white cardboard the Suzy Q came in. It's the size of a generic postcard. Waxy on one side, my pen won't take to it. But ink flows smoothly when I turn it over.

Young Abe loved to write. Anywhere he could. He practiced writing words in snow. In sand. In dust. He'd use ink made from copperas and blackberry root, and a turkey buzzard quill to write his name. Sometimes he'd write with charcoal. Before long he was writing letters for the family. And for folks who lived nearby.

Most people know the Gettysburg Address or the Emancipation Proclamation, but Lincoln wrote some fine personal letters too. And he loved to get mail. Sometimes it was the only thing that would cheer his gloomy self up.

I write on my generic postcard:

Dear Mr. Lincoln,

Your greatest ambition was to be esteemed by others. You did this by running for office. My greatest ambition was to run too. Not for office. But just to run. Across the prairie. And the valley. The desert and the oceans. Mr. Lincoln, I just love to run. But a cancer has taken my leg. I wouldn't have minded as much if I had had my go first. A bargain with time. You had your go. The presidency. If you could do it all over again, would you still trade your life for it? I believe I would trade mine for another four years of running.

Your friend,
Meghan Hartman

II.
Bankrupt

The Big Game

*L*ast May they suddenly appeared. Foreclosure signs on my favorite field. The Jacobs place. My heart was a wild leaping frog that morning. To think of Mr. Jacobs and his pear-shaped wife being driven to some decrepit trailer park with rock hard dirt and no grass. No room to grow anything. And I could not run when I thought of this and saw: **HARTMAN SAVINGS AND LOAN** in bold letters. Nailed to the wood posts that hold the barbed wire. Nailed to the porch of the white farmhouse. Nailed and screwed.

"The bank with a heart."

My family name. My family's bank until 1926, when my grandfather lost his shares in a poker game. Aces to royal flush.

People here don't take kindly to change. Especially where their money is concerned. So they kept the name the same.

The Banker has never forgiven my grandfather for the loss of all that could have been his. For years, he's been steadily buying back shares. Steadily and slowly. Soon the controlling interest will again be in our family. Don't ask me why. There's no one to inherit it. He's already given up on Killian. And thanks to those suits from Washington, he's got PJ destined for bigger things. As for me, I would've helped Mr. Jacobs out. Ha! Here's one for the tombstone: She bought the farm before she could give it back.

But I'm not going anywhere. No way. At least I hope not.

Debt

We're in good company. In one book I read that Lincoln had financial problems too. Bad luck beginning in his boyhood. His daddy, Tom Lincoln, lost three farms in Kentucky on account of land title problems. When Abe was seven, his sister and parents packed up and made their way to Indiana. Squatters. Built a cabin on land they didn't own. Then the wells ran dry. Not long after, his mama died from milk sickness, and Abe had to carve her coffin pegs. But he survived it all.

In New Salem, Illinois, he managed a store that went belly-up. Joined the militia the following year to fight in the Black Hawk War. His war earnings went into a partnership with a preacher's son who drank himself and the business to death. All the debt fell on Lincoln.

He tried surveying for a while. But because he couldn't pay off what he owed, the sheriff auctioned off his horse and instruments.

Most people would have given up. But he endured. Endurance is the sign of a champion.

Blue Ribbons

I won my first race when I was eleven. At the parks and recreation field day. End of summer picnic event. Sniffing the smell of lighter fluid and burnt hot dogs while volunteers pinned numbered paper plates to our backs.

No one in my age group came close. I won them all. The 50. The 100. The 440 dash. One of the volunteers was Mrs. Smithers, a public high-school track coach. She got me working out regularly with her high-school team. I learned. How to breathe. Stretch. Work starter blocks. Those days I was happy. The happiest kid in all of Illinois. Until the next year when my mother died. That's when running became my life.

Mrs. Smithers made you work hard. Still, when you'd done an okay job, you knew. Before long some track gossip caught up with the coach at St.

Catherine's. He offered me a full ride. Room and board, the whole fat hog. Thanks, no. I was happy with Mrs. Smithers.

Coach Cutter stayed and talked to the Banker a long time. That's how I ended up at St. Cats. The idea of living in a dorm in the same town where our house was seemed like a waste of money, but Coach liked keeping the whole team together. And besides, St. Cats had plenty of money to burn. But mostly it seemed like the Banker was trying to get rid of me. Like the conservative blue bloods from St. Louis who shipped their children there. Or those from the Chicago burbs.

St. Cats was nothing like other Catholic schools, which were struggling to survive. It had a fine clay track. And a new indoor gym, wider than a cornfield. A gym with weights and machines. All for girls. None of it had to be shared with boys.

After three years of pushing St. Cats as far as the state finals, Coach Cutter was determined to clinch it once and for all. That's where I came in. "Don't worry," he told me. "We can schedule your classes around training sessions. And you'll love the pool. Olympic size. Great for off-season workouts."

I looked at the two of them sitting on the couch like they had just closed a business deal. They had. My whole life was being planned and I didn't have a say-so. "It's a nice offer," I said cautiously, "but I've been training with Mrs. Smithers." I was torn up about it. Mrs. Smithers, her tiny energetic self in a jogging suit. A stopwatch around her neck. Seconds. Minutes. Days. Adding up to two years. Two years that she trained me even though I couldn't run with her team until I started high school.

"Meghan, can't you see what he's offering you?" These sorts of statements by the Banker seemed like questions but never were.

"I see," I said. I wondered if my mom would have taken my side. She liked Mrs. Smithers.

The coach didn't speak. He knew when to be silent.

The next day I went to see Mrs. Smithers and told her the whole sorry story.

"I don't want to see you go," she said.

Shoot. I looked down on the top of her curly black hair, trying not to cry.

In the end, Mrs. Smithers made it easy. "It's the best thing for your career," she said finally.

Career. At thirteen. I wondered who she was talking about.

Holy Cards

I stare at the food tray in front of me. "I'm not eating this crap."

"If you don't, you'll have to be fed intravenously with big needles." The redheaded sadist threatens me again. "And you won't like it."

I picture what my mashed potatoes will look like in her hair.

"Well . . ." she says, holding the tray lid and tapping her foot impatiently.

"Eat it yourself."

Her face reddens to match her hair. She exits in a huff. Off to write something complimentary on my chart, no doubt.

When I'm rid of her, Doctor Take More comes in to have a look. I can see his dark nylon socks sticking out from his pant legs. To tell you the truth, there's more personality in string beans. He pulls back the covers. "How are we doing today?" he asks.

"We?" I say. "Who is we?"

His cough is forced. Nervous.

"Oh yes, my stump and I. Why, we're just fine. Just hunky-damn-dory."

No response.

"You ought to get that cough checked out," I tell him.

He flashes a prescription smile, then beats a path out the door. No doubt about it: his bedside manner was ordered from a Sears catalog.

I shove the lunch tray out of my way. It glides across the room on its wheels, stops when it bumps into a corner chair. I roll on my side, open the night-table drawer, and take out my cigar box.

Mixed in with my pictures is a holy card. Well, it's not *really* a holy card. Not like the kind you get at funerals with pious figures rising up to heaven on a magic cloud. Flip those over and you'll find birth and death stats of the dearly departed along with a prayer to the Big Cheesus.

When I was a kid, holy cards were high status. Right up there with baseball cards. The basic Mary starter collection: Mary in a blue robe. Mary and Elizabeth after the Immaculate Conception. (No one could ever tell them apart even though Elizabeth was a million menopausal years older, but it didn't matter—you needed that card.) And you needed Mary weeping at the foot of the cross.

The Jesus starter pack was more complex. The early years: The flight to Egypt. A manger scene. The obedient son making furniture. The miracle-working period: Jesus churning out wedding booze. Or multiplying loaves and fishes. Raising the crusty dead lepers.

Most important were the final death days: The scourging at the pillar. Jesus carrying his cross. The crucifixion scene with both Marys weeping simultaneously—the good mother and the naughty prostitute.

Joseph was like a movie extra. He hardly ever made it into the collection except as a side character. Leading a donkey maybe.

Once you had the basic collection, you could begin trading extras or duplicates for the really good ones. Saint Stephen with arrows. Joan of Arc burning on the stick pile. Saint George chopping up the dragon. Find a little-known saint who met with a gruesome fate: that was as good as an early Mickey Mantle.

I had one of a Jesuit missionary after the Indians got hold of his tongue, and another saint at the peak of her stigmata. But they're gone now. All except this one: a black, white, and gray photograph of John Kennedy. It was a special thing to Catholics, him being the first Catholic president and all. Ushers put them in the pews Sunday after his funeral.

At school when we first heard he'd been shot, all

the sisters cried. We prayed for an hour. Then they called in the buses early and dismissed us. I ran all the way home to tell. My mother was sitting on the floor in front of the TV crying—her double-jointed knees and legs off to each side, Killian next to her. He was crying, too.

I knew it was a terrible terrible thing that happened, but I was only seven and didn't really understand. Not like you do when you're older. Still, it was a day I'd never forget. So I saved that card.

Post-Holy Card

I set down the JFK card for a second and fish in the box for a snapshot of my mom. She's holding half a dozen ice-cream bars—the big chocolate nut-covered ones—three in each hand. The photo was taken at the state fair one year when she went to hear Perry Como sing. She just loved Perry Como. And afterwards when the grounds were closing down for the night, some ice-cream vendor just gave them to her. There she was, with three huge bars in each hand, laughing and trying to figure out which one to bite into first. Seeing her so happy over ice cream suddenly makes me wonder about unhappiness.

What makes a person unhappy? Every day I live I understand a little more. I used to wear my Big Brownie Smile to keep that understanding to myself. *I have something in my pocket that belongs across my face* . . . I joined the Brownies, learned that song, the same year Kennedy was assassinated.

Of course that "something" is a Big Brownie Smile. People who knew my mom tell me all the time how much I look like her. But when I look in the mirror or at this photograph, I just don't see the resemblance. And since my leg took off down the road, I don't smile anymore unless I feel like it.

I put her picture away carefully, then pick up the holy Jack card once more and turn it over. There's nothing on the back of it, no prayers or anything. Just blank. I like that. I take out my pencil and start to write.

Dear Mr. Lincoln,

I am sending you a post-holy card of another president who was shot in the head like you. People say there were many similarities between his assassination and yours, but the real similarity is this: if you have a vision for something pure and good and a deep love inside you, you don't live long. Some butt-hole will kill you. If you're lucky you die. If you're not, you linger on like my brother Killian. The living dead. He was part of a terrible war in Asia that is just now ending.

When he came home, people spit on him.
We have been in a sorry state since
you left us.

Your one-legged friend,
Meghan Hartman

Rent-A-Leg

You want to hear something sorry? How about watching your stump shrivel up. Shrink the stump. Sounds like witch doctor medicine, but it's true. They shrink the stump. It makes a better fit for the fake leg. Sometimes they use devices—stump-shrinking socks. Shrink, shrink, shrink. Until it can fit right into the artificial limb. The shrinkers say it shouldn't take too long for sub-cutaneous fat to vanish because I'm a runner and have mostly muscle in my legs. Runner. Ha!

In the meantime it's Rent-A-Leg. They modify and replace parts. You rent them from the pros-thetist. A little weasely guy who guarantees his work-manship. Big deal. Where's the guarantee for the rest? I imagine his little shop of horrors in some dingy back alley with dirt-encrusted windows. Soon, if I'm a real good girl, I'll get my own permanent and genuine prosthesis, which will last about a year and a half. Probably longer than me.

In the meantime, why struggle with a poor plastic substitute? Crutches will do just as well.

The Banker

The Banker walks in, navy socks and matching suit. Gold pen in his breast pocket. He sits down on the vinyl chair.

"The nurse tells me you're not eating."

"The nurse doesn't know anything." She's just the kind of creep to sense a wedge between two people and kick it in deeper. "Try visiting on a week-day. Janey will tell you different."

He lifts the cover on the food and looks at the untouched meal. Runny mashed potatoes. Rubber pork chop. Jiggling Jell-O. For him, anything's better than looking at me. Fine then, I won't look at him either. But I do, out of the corner of my eye.

"All the same," he says, then covers the plate back up and sits down again. He's clean-shaven and attractive. The kind of man most women would love to sit next to on an airplane.

There are times I'd like to tell him some of what I feel. What I know. My letter from Georgy stuffed in one of his desk drawers. Give me my damn letter. But I don't say anything, to keep PJ in the clear.

"How's the pain today? Any better?" He looks to his right, at the stack of books.

"Compared to what?" To yesterday? To three days ago? To the last time he was here? Janey said he was at the hospital nonstop at the beginning. All through the surgery and for three days after. Wild horses couldn't drag him away. But I was too drugged to remember. Anyway, he probably would have been chewing me out if I was conscious. He was still fuming mad about St. Cats.

"I'm just asking if you're feeling better." He's farther away than the stars. A cold constellation on a bright winter night. The Big Disappointment. What we are to each other. We've grown another trillion light-years apart since my mom died. And now that I'm legless, he can't even stand to look at me.

"Just peachy. Want me to dance an Irish jig?"

"Meghan . . . " He starts but doesn't finish his sentence. It wouldn't seem very Christian of him to turn his back on me like this. So he comes. Right after Sunday Mass. What an upstanding citizen.

I Know Better

I pull the sheet over my head, cross my hands on my chest. Alright, let's just get the damn thing over with. How long do I have to wait around this dump for my other limbs to drop off? *Kiss me quick, there goes my upper lip. Leprosy.* Sang that when I was a kid.

I'm not forgetting Doctor Take More's "favorable prognosis." But doctors lie. And they make mistakes. You go in to have your tonsils removed and come out with one kidney. Two weeks later you're dead from infection or pneumonia. It's the nasty Brezhnev types with caterpillar eyebrows who live forever.

But Doctor Take More is quite certain. They think they got all the cancer. He even smiled encouragingly. Yeah right. Let someone cut off part of you. Your ding-dong, for instance. Then come in here and show me your Big Brownie Smile.

More about Doctors

I'm ungrateful. I know it. I should be thankful he saved my life. But that's just one more thing that makes me a terrible person inside. I'm not the least bit thankful for Dr. Take More and his power tools.

The most dreaded thing in the Civil War was doctors. Get a compound fracture from a gunshot and it was all over. Men would hide their condemned limbs from those butchers. Otherwise, they'd be hauled to the chop shop, a rag of chloroform shoved under their nose. After Shiloh, eight out of ten Confederate soldiers died from amputation surgery. That's what I read.

There's an oak box in the Springfield museum with surgeon's implements inside. If no one told you, you'd think you were looking at carpenter's tools. But they needed all those saws, because the rule was to chop off the limb within twenty-four hours. If you waited longer than that you were just about certain to die. Doctor Take More: the sooner the better.

What do you think they did with all those limbs? Outside Atlanta in the summer of '64, a soldier at a field hospital got throw-up sick when he found a pile of arms and legs behind a building. It was the worst horror of the whole war, he said.

Sometimes, doctors would do something even more gruesome. They'd take out the joint and leave the limb. It's what they called resection. What it really was: a dangling flap of worthless skin to remind you forever of what you no longer had.

I guess it could be worse. I could have been left with a hollow tube of flesh. Try running with a three-foot flipper.

Running into Georgy

*R*unning can transform you. Your body feels different. In a way it's like an electric discharge. Hop a couple of neighborhood fences with energy to spare. Keep going. Down the cinder alley to tree-lined sidewalks. Move fast. Don't step on cracks. Through a large open field near the hospital. Watch for glass bottles. Some days it's like that, a steady obstacle course. Eyes must move faster than legs. Rabbit hole, sprained ankle.

But it's dazzling to turn a final corner and catch the late sun glinting on chrome or shattering into a prism of color on a dull little spot of oil. To be finally spent, yet see everything around continue, can sometimes be comforting. The jabbing pain in my side becomes sweet as it fades. And the lines of sweat slow on my back and melt into the cotton of my shirt.

Once a coach gets ahold of you, all that changes.

Your body is heavy and leaden by the end of practice. You can't go on. But you have to.

Suck wildly for air and continue. Like everyone else. Around and around and around the track. Coach's voice, a singsong kind of music as I pass. It mingles with the pounding of feet. Spikes biting into cinder.

We train twice a day. In the morning and late afternoon. Stretch. Run a warm-up mile. Then Coach gives orders. Maybe timed sprints for speed. Or distance running for endurance. Or hand-off techniques on the 440 relay. A never-ending routine.

What I want is to cut loose. No holding back. But boring routine is part of what it takes to get there. To the top. That's where I was going. So fast. Easy college scholarship. Illinois, Indiana, California—they all were already scoping me out.

One morning practice ran late. I was hustling to make it to my 8:30 class, doing a balancing act. Glass of water. Glass of juice. Cup of coffee. All suddenly airborne. I plowed into Georgy with my breakfast tray. Orange juice all over her white oxford blouse. Only thing spared was the box of Rice Krispies crammed in my jacket pocket.

"This how you introduce yourself to all newcomers?"

"No, I—" I knew my face was turning red. She wasn't the least bit rattled. Down on the floor picking up glass. Couldn't help noticing how thin and nimble her fingers were. How gracefully she picked up the splintered pieces one at a time without touching any others next to them. And quickly too. I imagined her shuffling a pea under walnut shells. Lifting wallets from jean pockets. Any combination of street hustles performed during her year hiatus from school.

When my eyes caught her tattoo—a murky blotch on her forearm showing through the white of her uniform blouse—I sliced my finger on the last piece of glass.

Nearness of
Faraway Places

Two months later on a Saturday night. We're sitting on my bed watching an old Hitchcock movie and eating popcorn. Georgy's using chopsticks. Shoveling up one popped kernel after another. During a commercial she pauses. Inspects a puffed piece. "You ever notice how much popcorn looks like cumulus clouds?"

"I never lost sleep thinking about it," I say. Sometimes she'd just get like that, stuck on an idea that seemed to make a whole lot of sense to her alone. Reminded me of Lincoln when he first learned how to write his name. Couldn't get over it. Wrote it over and over like it meant something secret and important.

I stare at the television but don't really watch it. I get to thinking that maybe I *should* lose sleep over things like that. Connections and similarities. On the same long kite tail of life are strung little torn sheets of meaning—separate, yet one strand in the wind.

At the next commercial, we talk about holy cards. "You lie."

"I swear it's true," says Georgy. "I *never* had a holy card collection as a kid."

Hard to imagine. "Growing up Catholic and no cards."

"It's different out West. Anyway," she says, "they ought to put people like Ralph Nader and Gloria Steinem on them. Johnny Appleseed. People who tried to make a difference."

"Or maybe they should use places instead," I add. "Majestic ones." The movie comes back on but we keep talking.

"Mount Rushmore would make a nice holy card," says Georgy. "Imagine climbing down Roosevelt's face."

Like Cary Grant is trying to do right now on the screen. "No," she shouts.

Georgy's getting exasperated at his attempts. She's pointing with her chopsticks, telling him which way to go and how to maneuver. She has rock sense. I guess—living in a town like Boulder.

"Wow." I watch him slide all over in his Sunday shoes, trying to save the woman of his dreams. He's really screwing up.

"I can't stand it. What a nincompoop." Georgy

turns off the television, then sits back down on the bed next to me.

"Hey, I was watching that."

"Hey yourself." She pokes me in the ribs with her chopsticks.

"So tell me the truth. How wild was wild?"

"You mean how wild did I have to be to end up in the enchanted land of corn and soybeans?"

I nod.

"Not very. Just some pot and stuff. I think my mother was afraid I was going to end up pregnant or something."

Georgy with a big belly. I laugh.

Georgy laughs, too. "Me, pregnant! I want to climb mountains, not become one."

I can't imagine being pregnant. Maybe that's part of what stopped me with Donnie.

Georgy says, "Thank God for Trojans."

"The Greeks?" I know as soon as I say this I shouldn't have.

Georgy drops her chopsticks and starts choking on a kernel in her throat. Next, she's slapping her chest with an open hand. The pip shoots out like a BB and ricochets off of the TV screen.

"I was just kidding," I say.

"No you weren't." Georgy catches her breath and begins an oral dissertation on condoms.

"Okay, okay. So I don't know all the brand names already." At least I'm not like that kid I saw at a basketball game once who thought he'd found a balloon beneath the bleachers.

I lean over the side of the bed and snatch the chopsticks off the floor and hand them back to Georgy.

"Anyway, it's no big deal," she says.

But it was a big deal. I felt like a corn-fed country girl around Georgy. She knew a lot of stuff about boys and marijuana and the insides of tattoo parlors. Besides climbing, I guess that's what she'd been doing during her year off. Hanging out with older kids and her mom didn't like it. But she wasn't around to do much about it. Too busy with her shoe store. Marketing a new line. Active footwear: running shoes, hiking boots, sport sandals. Georgy's dad split when she was a baby. Left her and her mom for a diner waitress.

I watch as Georgy pinches the slender sticks between her fingers and chases the old maids around the bottom of the bowl.

"So," she says, "my mom's solution to all this was St. Cats, her alma mater." Georgy drops a blackened kernel into her mouth. It crunches hard when she bites down. Next, a bitter puckering of the lips. "No way was I going to come here but we struck a deal."

"A bribe! Let's hear."

"My last two years here with better grades for college, and a climbing trip right after graduation." Her mother promised Georgy she could go anywhere:

The British Isles. Australia and New Zealand. South Africa. Spain. But it was France she took a fancy to. The boulders of Fontainebleau. The Vercors near Grenoble. The Gorges du Verdon close to the Mediterranean. She rattles off the names of faraway places and it sounds like magic.

"Where else have you been?" I ask.

"The Philippines. Canada and Hawaii. All the states. Mostly on buying trips with my mom."

I ask her more about those places. She gives me a bored expression and yawns. But name a place that has rocks nearby, and then you'll hear all about their composition and features. Instead of telling you about food, clothes, or stained-glass windows, she'll tell you about chimneys—the cracks in the rock you sort of shimmy up—or overhangs, which jut out like roofs. Georgy would climb Jacob's ladder if it existed. Nonstop, all the way to heaven.

It's silly to think about it now, but we made plans. I'd spend the summer in Colorado with her. Just us, running and climbing and hollering into the wind. The altitude and the mountains. It would have been great, because I'd never traveled much. And I don't think I would have gotten homesick. Not with Georgy. Not as long as I could still run.

I'd like to travel more. Tibet. Martinique. Haiti. Egypt. I'd like to see Vietnam, too. For different reasons. See what kind of place turned my brother into a stranger. Or maybe I wouldn't. Maybe it's the last place in the world I'd want to go. The first place Killian ever went. The only place. A place that never really let him come home.

When Killian got back, he was thin and covered with mosquito bites. Like he'd been camping with his buddies at Grass Lake, and they hadn't bothered to eat. But that isn't where he'd been. At the dinner table he'd stare off into space. Traveling somewhere far away in his mind. No place we could ever know. It scared me.

The first week he'd shout in his sleep, waking everyone up. One night we found him under his bed. After that he took to going outside, walking the dark streets. He just couldn't stand the four walls. Said it was like being inside a shrinking elevator.

He's never slept a night indoors since. Not that I know of. And I'm scared he never will.

Advanced Training

At first, when Killian was drafted, we thought he'd get some other assignment. Maybe even sent to Germany. But after boot camp, Killian's military occupational specialty—what they called MOS—was an 11B. That stood for infantry training, and it meant he might as well start packing his bags for Vietnam. It knocked the breath out of all of us. Even though we knew from the beginning there was a good chance he'd get sent.

I had had a bunch of old war movie scenarios in my head, safe ones: Killian behind a typewriter, or peeling potatoes—a four-foot pile in front of him. If not this, then driving a truck, or maybe working on the *Stars and Stripes*. Never once did I picture him as a soldier.

Advanced training was a lot like basic: the difference, Killian wrote to Janey, was that you had no hope of becoming a truck driver, cook, or mechanic. You were going to specialize in killing.

In boot camp the enemy was Charlie, or the VC. They'd march and sing "I want to go to Vietnam. I want to kill a Vietcong." Now, in advanced training, the Vietcong were gooks, dinks, zipperheads, or slopes, and everything became Kill Kill Kill. Killian would shove his bayonet into some dummy and the drill sergeant would yell at him to spike it harder. Hell, he said, with your damn name, you're halfway there.

His drill sergeant wasn't much different from the basic-training one, except that Killian had begun to like him. He had already been to Vietnam and was decorated. Killian listened to what he said. Repeated phrases in his head like pop lyrics. Hung on to them like his life depended on it. And it did.

Killian came to believe, even before setting foot on the soil, that you couldn't trust a single gook. Not women. Not children. Not babies. They'd try to poison your food, piss in your Coke cans, or drop a grenade right next to your foot. Even the soil was sinister. Punji pits and bombs everywhere.

His world had begun to change and he changed right along with it, ever eager to please. Now desperate to survive.

To Talk or Not to Talk

I've lost track of how many candy bars I've eaten today. Five or six wrappers are stuffed in the Kleenex box on my nightstand. Who cares if I turn into the Goodyear blimp? Make up for lost leg weight. I'm eating a Bit-O-Honey, the tan taffy pulling at my teeth like rubber bands on braces. Outside my window is the melancholy time of day— dusk, when drivers turn on their headlights and birds stop singing. I'm shoving another hunk of taffy into my mouth when PJ comes through the door.

"How many?" I ask. She's later than usual.

She pulls off her mittens. I watch her little fingers wiggle. "Two shots of novocaine. I hate that worse than the filling." She shoves the mittens into the pocket of her coat, then takes it off and stuffs it in the corner chair along with her book bag.

She reaches for a piece of the taffy.

"No, PJ." I grab it back. "That could pull out the filling."

She puts a hand to her cheek and sighs. "What else is there?"

"How about a peppermint patty?"

"No, that smells too minty like the dentist's office."

I pull open the nightstand drawer. "A strawberry Sno-Ball then. That should be okay."

"Yes, a Sno-Ball." She claps her hands together. A crooked smile shoots up one side of her face.

"I would have saved more for you, PJ, but I kind of got carried away." Sam had to go out of town for a couple of days. Some nut cracker convention in Milwaukee. They probably hand out shrunken little heads on key chains. Not that I care. But then I think about him being gone and something flip-flops in my chest.

"This is fine," she says. "One of my favorites."

Not mine. I feel kind of bad leaving all my least favorite candy for PJ. "You know," I say, "I think a person can get through anything with a good supply of candy."

"Ummm." She nods in agreement. Little shreds of coconut pearl on her lip.

I polish off the last rectangle of taffy.

"Oh, I just remembered. I found something of yours under my bed."

"You tackled the underworld?"

"Had to. We got a mouse upstairs. Mrs. Blanch said if I didn't clean under there, she'd send in the city health department."

I unwrap the newspaper, pull out a musical figurine. A porcelain hobo. Mushroom-brown eyes and bright patches on his pants. Slung over his shoulder is a stick. A red bandanna bundle is tied to the end of it.

"Wow, I'd forgotten about this." A present from my mom after Pop Kelley died. I wind it up and set it on the hospital tray. I watch it slowly turn in circles to the tune of "Raindrops Keep Falling on My Head."

"I loved it so much," says PJ. "I used to go in your room and play it when you weren't there, but then one day I knocked it over." She looks at me, the lines of worry wrinkling her forehead. "I tried to glue it back together, but I felt so bad that I just hid it underneath the bed."

"I wondered what happened to this."

"Are you mad, Meghan?"

"No. That's all right." With my finger I trace a thin glue line around Johnny's neck. "He was always kind of sad anyway."

"I know," she says.

We watch until the last little note hangs in the air and the hobo finally stops turning.

"Meghan," she says. "Do you think Dad will let me keep the mouse if we catch it?"

Probably not. Suddenly I think about him

opening my mail and I get mad all over again. Finders keepers. "Who cares what he wants."

"You and Dad are still really mad at each other, aren't you?"

"Doesn't take a microscope to see that one," I snort.

"Is it because of what happened at school? No one will tell me. Did you do something really bad, Meghan?"

I think about what really bad means. "Not like John Wilkes Booth," I say.

PJ doesn't push the St. Cats incident any further, but she zeroes in on the Banker and me again. "But you were mad at each other before, for a long time. Once you didn't speak to each other for a month. Remember that, Meghan? I had to play the radio just to hear someone talk to me."

"I talked to you, PJ."

PJ nods. "But at the dinner table no one would ever say anything. I don't remember why."

"That was a long time ago."

PJ nods again.

I try to think of an easy way to explain it to her but there really are no shortcuts. "You know, when Mom died things changed. They used to argue stuff out. Now he calls all the shots." Me dumped at St. Cats. Killian pushed into the arms of the enemy.

"But now you won't talk to your friend Georgy either."

"That's different," I say.

PJ puts on her coat. I watch the wooden buttons one by one slide through her fingers until she is completely wrapped in blue.

"Meghan," she says, "will you ever quit talking to me?"

"Never," I say. "Not in a million years."

She smiles and slips out the door. In the hallway, I hear the rumble of the dinner cart rolling off of the elevator.

Chicken and Egg

When PJ goes I reach underneath my pillow and pull out my rosary. I spin it like a lasso, then let it wrap around my index finger, a miniature tetherball pole. I never pray on it, but I keep it around as sort of a good luck charm.

People have been known to sleep with all sorts of strange things underneath their pillows: wedding cake, teeth, guns. So even though it's kind of superstitious on my part, it doesn't exactly seem like I'm the only fool out there. And who knows? What if it could be a really good thing? Just believing something will help can make it work. Look at how the measly French army kicked butt with Joan of Arc up there on a horse.

Sometimes I talk to my mom even though she's not here anymore. But then, if you're talking to the person in your mind, isn't it like they *are* here? Or does something have to exist outside of you to be real? The Big Cheese upstairs, for instance. I wonder if this is considered one of those chicken and egg questions, which I might have been able to figure out. If I had gotten to take that philosophy class I signed up for before I was excommunicated. Now I'll be just a Know-Nothing on the subject. Ha!

The Know-Nothing party was an anti-Catholic hate group alive and kicking in Lincoln's day. Lincoln said if they ever got control of the country, he'd rather move to Russia. Not that he was Catholic. Hell, he didn't belong to any religion, although plenty claimed him after his death. His wife said he was not a "technical Christian." I like that.

Someone once gave him a Bible when he was feeling down. He said it was the best cure for the blues if you could just believe it was the truth. *If* is a big word.

I'm keeping the rosary anyway.

Lincoln's Sadness

When I first read about Lincoln and his depression I was almost happy. It made him more perfect. I know that's not too logical but what I mean is, the pedestal was getting pretty tall. Our greatest president with emotional termites. You can't get much more real than that.

Lincoln had terrible bouts. Some days he was afraid to be around knives for fear of what he might do. He once told a friend that he never dared carry a pocketknife, although he carried one the night he was shot.

Still, he had plenty of things to be sad about even before becoming president. Frontier loneliness, the cold, the hunger. There's hardly a more lonesome place in winter than the Midwest. Fields are stretched out and bare. Spindly trees bent over with the weight of ice. And when you see the lean crows so still they look frozen in place on the gray wintry snow, it's enough to make you howl at the skies.

Lincoln's mom died when he was nine, his sister when he was a teenager, and once he almost died when he was kicked by a horse. These hurtful things he never forgot. He married and lost two sons. He struggled to keep from losing a whole nation.

Women made him feel awkward and melancholy. He'd get sad and brood over them and folks said he was a lot like Old Mord, his uncle, who was full of life one moment and gloomy the next. There were other Lincolns too who would go from laughing to down-in-the-dumps-bottom-of-the-barrel spells of pure sadness. Another chicken and egg: who knows how much you make on your own and how much is dealt to you from the plastic-coated gene deck? Joker with one eye. Queen without a heart.

Today, you can be a politician if you cheat on your wife, your taxes, and your diet. You can be greedy, you can lie, you can drink too much. But if you are a politician and admit to sadness, you'll be dropped like a hot potato, the way Senator Eagleton was.

A man like Lincoln could never be president today. A man like Lincoln today maybe wouldn't wait to have a gun pointed at him. He'd probably do it himself.

No Pills

It's close to midnight when Janey comes in my room. I hear the sound of her panty hose rubbing together as she walks over to my bed. I lie on my back with my eyes wide open.

"Meghan," she says. She slides her hand into mine and squeezes lightly. "Do you want something to help you sleep?"

"No," I tell her. "It leaves me groggy and with no memory of dreams." The only reason to sleep is to hope for the running dream again. The running dream. Running.

The Pain of
Getting Started

Always when I begin to run the wind whistles in my ears like in an ocean shell. Cold and painful at first. But as the miles pass I don't feel anything except for the throb of blood pumping through me. Veins and arteries. To and from the heart. Like so many little Venetian canals gone crazy. A whole city is at work inside me and a whole country is spread out before me. Within an hour's run I can be almost anywhere: edge of the interstate that slices through soybean fields, or in the heart of town where Lincoln relics still abound. Sometimes I run past the old churches and taverns, wondering who has a more loyal following.

I can find my way to the great contemporary landmarks, too: Putt-putt golf course. The mall. The boat marina. And I am part of all of this—history and plastic present, moving in and out of my vision. This is no one-horse town anymore.

I think about all kinds of things and sometimes I think about nothing and ten miles have passed when a cramp in the arch of my foot breaks my trance. I work it out and then taper off for the day.

They say you can learn to run with an artificial leg. That's what they say, but in truth I have a better chance of seeing the world through a glass eye than truly running with an artificial leg.

Genuinely Artificial

At first everyone wants to tell you all the things a mechanical leg can do for you. With all the enthusiasm and believability of used-car salesmen on the local TV station. Kevin in his plaid pants.

"As good as perfume," he jokes, and shoots deodorant into the air. Kevin is my physical therapist.

"Get out of here. No way am I going to use that stuff." Another goddamn thing no one told me about. They don't tell you how much harder you have to work just in order to walk. Or that the phony limb makes you sweat more and can cause lesions from rubbing against the stump. But soon enough you learn. Never rubbing alcohol. Use cornstarch or baby powder. Shake some into the socket.

"It's not so bad," he says.

"For you," I say. "You go home and put both your

feet up on an easy chair, swill beer and watch Johnny Carson through your toes."

"Come on, Meghan."

"Just forget it," I shout.

There's other things too. Your sweat glands can get clogged, causing boils and cysts and all kinds of junk to pop out on what's left of your leg. And there's all kinds of pressure and stress problems too. "I'm not wearing this goddamn thing."

I hurl the Rent-A-Leg across the PT room. It lands in the bubbling whirlpool bath, an odd incongruous thing. Fly in soup. Fingernail in applesauce.

"Meghan!" Kevin's fishing the leg out of the bubbly.

"I want my own leg back," I yell. I pick up my crutches and make for the door. "Not some rented piece of shit."

If I Were a Saint

By now, I imagine, my leg has shriveled and decomposed. Unless of course it's in a big jar of alcohol-like specimens from biology class: frog, fetal pig, Meghan's leg.

If I were a saint, my leg wouldn't decompose. Take Saint Bernadette, for example. A hundred years under glass looking fresh as yesterday's death. Or Saint Bonaventure's head, which had a livid life as well until it disappeared during the French Revolution.

A nondecaying corpse is one criterion of sainthood. They checked Old Abe out pretty good. (Although for supposedly different reasons.) Opened his casket four times. Mostly to make sure it was him inside. The last time in 1901. Once there was even a plot to steal the body from the tomb. Use his relics as ransom. But no one ever said what he looked like.

A fine saintly specimen or just bones?

I think of all those people out in California who have themselves frozen before death, hoping for a cure. Even if my leg made it to some freezer out there and they found a cure—say fifty years from now—what good would the leg of a sixteen-year-old do for me, frozen or thawed.

Love of Perfection

A chilly October day, but sunny. The leaves were a million different shades of color. Red. Green. Orange. Yellow. Brown. No clouds in the sky. Lots and lots of light.

Georgy was up at dawn, knocking on my door. Three or four ropes hung over her shoulder and some hooks and links and junk like that, which clanged together when she walked. "You going to sleep all day?"

I rolled over and looked at the clock. Six-fifteen on a Saturday morning. I made growling noises and pulled the covers up over my head.

"Come on, sleepyhead. Up and at 'em."

"You're deranged. Go away." I pulled the covers tighter.

"You promised we'd go to the gravel pit again. Come on, Meghan, I'm dying for a climb. If we don't get out of here, I'll be scaling the bell tower."

"Are you crazy?" I had caught her staring at it more than once.

The sun was up when we got to the old quarry, which helped warm things up a bit. I sat on the ground with a cup of coffee, my back resting against a rusty fifty-gallon drum. Stray machinery had been left at random—trucks and dozers—like toys in a sandlot. I was sure we were trespassing, but it was the only place I could think of where a person might climb something other than a tree.

I watched Georgy uncoil and test her ropes, excited as a birthday kid. "Come on. You want to climb?"

"I'm not even awake yet. I'm just perfecting the vertical REM pattern."

"Oh, God, I love the morning," said Georgy. "It's so invigorating."

I slurped my coffee.

"You're hopeless, Hartman."

"Hey, I climbed the last two times with you, didn't I?" I never knew there were so many muscles and tendons in the hand, and every one of them was sore for days afterwards. I looked at my fingers wrapped comfortably around my coffee cup. No way.

"Come on. It was a piece of cake for you."

"Says who?" I took another drink of coffee and scratched my back against the metal drum like a waking bear.

Georgy surveyed the quarry. Layered rows where rock had been cut deep into the earth. I was watching her and trying to come up with an original idea for my term paper in English, and getting nowhere. Lincoln was an easy choice for history, but English . . .

Soon I forget all about it as I watch Georgy. She's busy concentrating. Studying the bluff, planning her moves. It's cool and dry. "I'm not chalking my hands today. The limestone is soft," she explains.

She grabs on and blends in. Stray black hairs poke out of her helmet and dance around her head in the breeze. Moments later the immediate details disappear. She's too high for me to see, so I imagine the intensity on her face. Narrow beam of concentration, eyes half-lidded in defiance toward sun and rock. Then I lose all that to the distant perspective and watch. Georgy climbs as though she were put on this earth to do nothing else. Her legs balanced, flexing to accommodate each new foothold. They're good legs. Strong like a runner's.

I knew then that I loved her. For that moment. For the beauty she gave me by doing a simple thing so perfectly.

Candy Blues

*P*J brings more candy. Tootsie Roll. Milky Way. Two more PayDays. A pack of Hostess Twinkies. We split the Twinkies first. She's going to break hers in half. Suck the tube of white cream from the center.

PJ doesn't look at me. Something's wrong. I wait for her to bring it up. She licks the white frosting off her lips. "I ran into Mrs. Smithers. She always asks about you, Meghan."

"Tell her I said hi."

"You want her to visit? She said she'd—"

"NO!"

PJ braces herself against the chair, startled by my shouting.

"No," I say more softly. "Not now." I'll think of track when I see her. Then I'll think about running. All the things I can't do anymore. On top of that, what would

I say? I change the subject. "What's new at school?"

"Nothing."

"You're awful sad-looking for nothing new."

"I got the blues a little," she says.

"Because?" I unwrap the Tootsie Roll, toss PJ a few segments.

"The mouse," she says. "They caught the mouse. Snapped its little head off in the trap." PJ starts to cry. "I wanted to take care of it, Meghan."

"I'm sorry, PJ," I say.

"Dad said I couldn't keep it. But they didn't have to *kill* it. They have those traps at the hardware store that catch them alive, but Dad said they cost too much, and then you still have the mouse to deal with."

"PJ, please don't cry or I might cry too." If I could I'd run to the pet store or a grain silo and catch her a mouse. A little one with soft whiskers.

"I'm sorry." She sniffs and runs the back of her hand along her nose.

"It's okay, PJ." I wish I could say something more hopeful, but my pockets are empty of those coins. We chew our candy in silence for the next couple of minutes.

"Listen, I've got an idea. You know my lucky socks?"

"The white ones with the clovers on them?"

"Yeah, those. They're in the second drawer of my dresser at home, the sock drawer. Folded inside the toe is a ten-dollar bill. Take it and go to the hardware store and get that trap. We'll catch us another mouse."

"You mean it, Meghan?"

"Absolutely. Mice are social. If there's one, there's others around. Get that trap and put some peanut butter in it."

"Not cheese?"

"No, they like peanut butter better. Put peanut butter in there and stick it under your bed."

"Okay."

"There's an old aquarium in the basement. You can use that for a home."

"I want to do it right now," says PJ.

"Well get moving then." Inside I'm fuming. How could he do that to her?

She jumps off the bed and reaches for her coat. She pulls the mittens out of the pockets and a thin stack of postcards comes with them scattering across the floor. "Oh, I forgot," says PJ. "Here's the post-cards you asked for."

"Thanks," I say. "That's great."

When PJ leaves, I call the Banker at work. His secretary puts me on hold. I rehearse my speech.

Another minute passes and she's back on the line. "He's busy," she tells me. Do I want to leave a message?

"I want to talk to him now."

"I told you, Meghan, he's in a meet—"

"I don't care if he's having cheese and crackers with the Twelve Apostles. Get him on the line now."

For the next thirty seconds, I listen to Muzak. Then he picks up the phone.

"What's wrong, Meghan?"

"You. You're what's wrong."

I hear him exhale. "Meghan." Now he's mad. "I'm very busy right now. I'll call—"

"You're always busy," I shout. "How could you kill it in front of her?"

"Just calm down, Meghan. What are you talking about?"

"You could have turned it loose in a field or at least thrown it out before she got up."

"Oh for Christ sakes, the mouse? You got me out of a meeting for a mouse? We'll discuss this later."

"Yeah, right." I'm so mad I could spit fire. "And another thing. Stealing someone else's mail is a federal offense." I slam down the receiver.

Once upon a time we were a happy family.
Or were we?

Leave Before Going

*I*n his uniform he was the most beautiful thing. A blend of boy and man. Brother and gleaming brass. He seemed taller. Beyond my reach. Around him was an air, a golden light of confidence. At the airport Killian lifted me off the ground. I felt electrified. To have him for two whole weeks before he left for Vietnam. All that mattered were those two weeks. Then he set me down and I was alone watching as he danced Janey around in circles kissing her in ways that made me happy. Jealous. Curious. All these things rolled into one.

I was still thinking of that shining moment long after he had changed into his civvies and sat on the back porch swing with Janey. And how seeing him so beautiful again I might actually lose him. To a foreign place with foreign names for reasons I did not understand. This gnawed at me. Squirrel on a corncob. Until my nerves were raw. I said how wrong I thought the war was.

He didn't answer. Didn't chime agreement like he used to. Even Janey was silent. Killian shifted the ankle of his left foot over his right knee and sipped on his PBR in a can.

The Banker had bought the Pabst Blue Ribbon as a sort of peace offering. Man to man. And because Killian was "old enough to die, but not old enough to buy," as everyone used to say. The Banker had a swallow or two, then disappeared until supper. Off in his tower with the *Wall Street Journal.*

"You could still go to Canada," I said. "I'll go with you."

Then Janey chimed in softly. "Don't you see, Meghan, he's stuck. He's just stuck and you're making it worse."

It never occurred to me before. Not like that. He was stuck. Stuck real tight and no choice was all right or all wrong. I thought of plastic green army men I used to line up in the dirt—how we'd knock over all the Germans in their silly-looking helmets and drab gray uniforms. One clump of soil thrown. Instant dirt-clog death. Rat-aaaa-tat-tat from our mouths. Things were good and bad then. Black and white. No gray. Now there's more and more gray. Maybe it's the wars that have changed, or maybe it's me, getting older.

"Don't worry," he said. "I'll be back."

But I did worry. I couldn't help it.

The next two weeks seemed to fly. Killian out with his many friends. And with Janey. He drank more beer than anyone I'd ever seen. And then one bleary-eyed morning, he disappeared. Away from the green-and-brown patchwork of the corn and wheat fields below. His shiny and beautiful boy self up into the clouds.

Holding Pen

*C*ow slaughter. It's a sickening thing to watch.
One at a time down a ramp, a bullet between
the eyes. The other cows don't see it but they hear it
and know their turn is coming. The butchers try to
prevent this because when cows get scared and their
adrenaline is pumping, well, it makes the meat tough.

That's what Oakland Army Base was for Killian.
A holding pen. There was really nothing to do
except wait. He fell out of his bunk twice a day—
along with hundreds of other men—waiting for his
name to be called. Day five: Killian Hartman.

Next he was locked up with all the others whose
names were called. Locked up in a humongous airplane hangar. A makeshift bunker with beds. Junk
food and phones. Two more days in the holding pen.
Next, to Travis Air Force Base. He and others like
him moved down the ramp leading toward the plane.

Leaving on a Jet Plane

All the 707s were stripped of their first-class pizzazz. Filled to capacity with soldiers bound for Nam. On one of those flights was Killian. Writing his first letter home. After they had landed to refuel in Guam. I think he was drunk. He kept repeating how numb his butt felt. Numb and drunk and being hurled five hundred miles an hour toward some hole I couldn't even pronounce.

Guys were talking trash to the flight attendants. Not the guy sitting next to Killian. He was reading from a pocket-sized Bible. In the back was a picture of his new baby girl. Taken when she was ten minutes old, all shriveled and pink. Sent Express Mail. Born while he was in the holding pen with Killian. Never got to touch his own baby. "The army is sorry enough if you die," he told Killian, "but couldn't give a shit about life."

Shoes

The next day PJ brings me a package. She struggles to pull it out of her school book bag. "It's from your friend in Colorado. Aren't you going to open it?"

"Not now, I'd rather talk to you."

"Well," she says, "I got the trap. The directions weren't very good, but I figured it out. It's under my bed now. But so far, no takers."

"Just be patient."

"I know, Meghan. I can hardly wait." She sets the package on the nightstand and sits down. "I'm sorry about the other day. You know, crying and everything."

"Sometimes we cry about little things because it's too hard to cry about big things. At least that's what Sam says."

"You like Sam, Meghan?"

"His socks don't match and he tells stupid jokes. He wears a yarmulke, too. But I think it's mostly to cover the bald spot on his head."

"I like hats," says PJ. "They wear hats in all the old movies and they look so suave."

"Suave is a good word." Not worth much in Scrabble, though, because it has three vowels.

"Yes, now watch me put on my hat and take my suave self home." PJ picks up her beret and pulls it down until it's resting on her nose.

I laugh out loud.

She pushes her hat back on her head, cocking it to one side. I admire her in the afternoon light. She's genuine. I think about that day on the ice pond. How different it would be if someone tried to take her hat now.

When she leaves I pick up the letters from my bedside table. Been sitting there since the other day. How to tell her what I've lost. How? I trace the blue border of the envelopes before putting them in my cigar box.

I stare at the package, shake it a couple times. It makes me smile. Just like Georgy to send rocks, a reminder of the summer we had planned. Though the box is kind of light. Curiosity gets the better of me and I pull off the wrapping. Inside is a fancy pair of running shoes made by her mom's company. White and maroon suede. Neon green laces; Georgy's contribution, I'm sure. I pick up a shoe, pull the wad of tissue paper from the toe and stick my hand inside. I lean forward, smell the new leather. It's the most spectacular pair of shoes I've ever seen. Then I remember where I am. And what I am. The shoe drops from my hand, back into the box. I pick up something else.

Too late to stop myself. The stainless steel pitcher flies through the television glass. Strike two.

III.
Legs

Paper Whites and
Look-Alikes

Sam looks at the shattered hull on the wall, then back at me.

"*Star Trek*. I hate that show."

"*Star Trek* my ass. What was in the package?"

"Running shoes. From Colorado."

"I see." He sits down on the bottom of the bed. "This raises a couple of issues, doesn't it?"

"It doesn't raise diddly."

"You've got to tell her."

"I don't have to tell her anything."

"It's not about her. It's for you, Meghan."

I get a feeling that part of what Sam's saying to me is true, but I don't want to hear it. Not one bit. "Our plans are shot to hell now and I'm not answering any damn letters."

The silent tactic again.

"Well. Just what am I supposed to say? Sorry I

139

can't drop by this summer. I'm short a leg." Georgy. The one good friend I'll possibly ever make in what's left of my life.

"It's never easy," says Sam.

"What do you know about it?" I snarl.

"I know she's important to you."

"So's my leg," I say, "but you don't see it hanging around anywhere."

"That's the scary part, isn't it? Wanting those we love to accept us for who we are. For what we've become."

"Tell that one to the Banker. First Killian, then me. PJ is the last one waiting to be crossed off his list."

"He hasn't crossed you off his list, Meghan."

"He can't even stand to look at me." For God sakes, I'm the kind of girl who keeps her money in her sock.

"Why do you think that is?"

"You tell me," I say. "You're supposed to be the one with all the clues."

"Well, let's start with the easy part, your appearance."

I cross my arms and lean back on my pillow. Missing leg. Big revelation.

"You look a lot like your mother."

"You too?" Another person who sees what I don't. I uncross my arms and grab the metal rails on either side of the bed.

"At least from the pictures you've shown me, and from what Janey says."

"Janey. You talk to Janey about this?"

"No, Meghan. What you and I discuss here is confidential, you know that. It came up casually."

"Like the weather," I snort.

"Yeah, like the weather," he says.

"She happened to mention how much you look like your mother. She says you've got your mother's temper and sense of humor too. Would you agree?"

I don't know how to answer that. I don't even look like myself anymore.

"Well, I'll take your silence to mean you're not in complete disagreement. Did you ever think how hard it was for your dad to lose your mom so suddenly? Then bam. A few years later you're sick too."

"He was mad at me before I got sick."

"He's lived through a lot of losses. That leaves people without reserves, particularly if they have no one to turn to."

I think of Killian and see red. "He pushed Killian, made him go."

"Don't you think he knows that?"

For a moment I feel like I'm seeing right into Sam's voice, seeing sadness in him for all of us. Suddenly I imagine Sam hugging me and me soaking his lopsided tie with my tears. I feel my face go red with embarrassment.

"Your dad was here around the clock after your

operation, Meghan. What does that tell you?"

I collect myself. "I was out like a light. What the hell difference did it make?"

Sam half smiles but doesn't say anything. I glare at him. I hate it when he knows he's got me thinking.

"We can talk about it more later," he says, "if you'd like."

I don't say anything. I'm busy watching a bobby pin worm its way south of Sam's yarmulke. Soon it will ping softly on the floor.

"I see you got some more flowers," he says.

"Paper whites. They stink."

"Who are they from?"

Jesus he's nosy. "Donnie."

Sam wiggles his forefinger and I can't help but smile.

"Yeah, Donnie with the lawn-mower finger." The box of butter mints. My first true love. When he came back to town to visit last year we didn't exactly go all the way, but close enough.

"Meghan?"

No way am I going to give him all the sordid details. For starters, Donnie wasn't a very good kisser, poking his big fat tongue in my mouth. I stop myself short of remembering the rest of the unpleasantness. He kept writing and calling when he got back home but I never answered. I felt bad. It meant something to him. Next time, if there is a next time, I'll opt for a pianist or someone whose hands don't belong to a rugby player like Donnie. But still, the smell of the flowers makes me feel bad and I wonder now, given everything, if we should have broken open the Trojan.

"Is there anything else you want to tell me?" he asks.

"Take the flowers with you. Please."

Malingerers

Just when things begin to improve with Sam he pisses in the fan: "Still refusing physical therapy?"

"What's the point?"

"In walking? In getting around in the world? You tell me, Meghan." He snatches the crutches from the wall. Makes a point of slapping them on the bottom of the bed. "You don't want to wear a prosthesis, fine. Keep hobbling around on these. And while you're at it you can start coming to my office. Tomorrow. Third floor."

"The hell with you." Just like that. Mr. Change of Plans. Expects me to drag my handicapped self to his door.

"I'm not asking you to do it for me," he says on his way out.

"Right," I say. "For my wonderful self."

"That's right, Meghan. For your wonderful self." The door swooshes shut behind him.

It used to be when I was scared I knew I could always run. But what do I do now? White mouse in the snake cage. I feel horribly sick inside. I'd like to stand in the shower and shave all my hair down to the skin. Take off everything inside and out. Find a way to open a door so the scared bird that flutters around inside my rib cage can escape.

There was a guy on Killian's squad so afraid of going back out on patrol that he shot himself in the foot. Killian said there were plenty of times he felt like doing the same. Instead he quit taking his malaria pills. Drank stream water without iodine tablets, hoping for some kind of jungle infection. All he got was more tired and sick-feeling. No discharge. But to shoot your own foot! To be so afraid it turns into some kind of crazy courage. At least the guy could have taken off his boots. Given them to a needy buddy. Chicken feet. Pass 'em on.

In the Civil War, they thought all they'd have to do was ditch their boots. No boots, no battles. But it didn't work that way. Being shoeless was no excuse. So men with bare bloodied feet trudged through the snow. Except for the gimps, those one-leggers like me. If they survived, they got to go home and deal with their own private war.

I look at the crutches on the bottom of my bed. With my good leg I kick them off, let them fall like pick-up sticks. This is my private war. No beauty, no glory here.

Thinking Back

*H*ow can I tell Georgy I'll never use these shoes? What would she think? Or say? To imagine her face as she sees this. Her forehead crinkled in disgust. Her eyes drawn in tight and close at the sight of mutilation. The mountains are only for the trim and the fit. No. No way.

I think about a time before Georgy when life at St. Cats was dismal. Nothing but girls with attitude and money to burn. Money without a second thought. Like Betsy Ballesteros, whose grandfather had made a fortune in plastics. Gutta-percha. Bakelite. Anything you could pour and mold. Betsy grew up the plastic queen with a nose for money. She knew where everybody's came from and how much they had. And until she gave the green light, I was stuck on lonely street. I ate my meals at a table by myself, listening to the whispers and laughter a few feet away. Feeling the stares.

Betsy would study my faded bell-bottoms and sockless Docksides. My wrinkled cotton shirts. The wire rims I wore for reading. Two weeks of this, then she comes up to me. Wants to know where I learned the art of understatement. Then she laughs and calls me a card. I never heard anybody talk like that. A card. Like something out of an old movie. That night there I was sitting at a table with half a dozen rich girls, smiling but still feeling something akin to loneliness inside.

Betsy liked you just fine if you had some money or social connections, but not more than her. The daughter of a loan officer on scholarship. Hardly a threat. Betsy and Georgy were another story. They hated each other from the first. In a way you could say it was the first worm in a can full of them with me wiggling around somewhere in the middle. The thing was, Betsy never did like Georgy—her clothes, her haircut, especially her tattoo—but when she found out Georgy truly couldn't care less, she desperately wanted to be her friend. Like everything in Betsy's life—if she couldn't have it, she wanted it. But I didn't hate her the way Georgy did. Betsy just couldn't help herself.

She was always primping in her mirror, afraid to have a hair out of place. Or an earring twisted. A smear of mascara showing was catastrophic. Once I stopped by Betsy's room on my way to the dining hall. Her eyes were all teared up. She had worn a new jacket all day long with the price tag hanging from the armpit and no one had told her.

If it were anybody else I would have burst out laughing, but Betsy looked so devastated with her elbow high in the air, pointing to the source of her sorrow.

I looked at the tag. Three jackets I could have bought for that same price. "It's not like it came off the JCPenney sale rack, Betsy. What's the big deal?"

"You don't understand." She dropped her arm and turned away. Then she burst into tears and I watched her shoulders shake.

She was right. I didn't understand then. It took a while for me to figure out that Betsy couldn't feel okay unless she had the appearance of perfection. To see her always look so good but feel like horse hockey inside . . . well, how can you hate a person like that?

Tomatoes and Virgins

If you put too much manure on tomatoes the vines become long and spindly and the tomato, when it finally comes, rots at the bottom. You put it in a dish with other tomatoes and it tries to destroy them too.

Big surprise. On the surface there were no rotten tomatoes in the Ballesteros home, because they have a full-time gardener and a greenhouse where they grow pale pink tomatoes in winter. The one sore spot was her mom, whom Betsy never talked about since the day she divorced Mr. Ballesteros to marry an Arab oil sheik and moved to Iran. That was the talk at school, anyway.

I had dinner at her house once on a cold February night, at a table longer than a bowling alley. Betsy and me at one end. Mr. Ballesteros at the other. When the sherbet came, I said how swell it was to have dessert in the middle of the meal so you could enjoy it without being too full. That cracked old Mr. B. right up. He called me a card. Asked Betsy wherever did she find me. Then he took me into the plastic museum of his study. Flamingoes. Miniature-corn corn-on-the-cob holders. Clear toilet seats with glitter and seashells. Everything his company had made over the years. I left with a yard virgin. A three-foot blue-and-white Madonna. A lightbulb up her gown.

In my room she glowed in the dark and by the end of the year I was quite fond of her. But Georgy was always messing with that statue. Used to hang her hat on Mary's outstretched arms. Once she put a cigarette between the fingers. I never objected. But somewhere in my Catholic schoolgirl head was the voice of a very old nun, her arthritic pointer finger in my face, telling me I'd pay for this sacrilege. And so would Georgy.

One evening when I had left Mary electrified too long, the bulb shifted and leaned toward the rear of her cape. It caused a large brown discoloration. Georgy made an endless variety of remarks. With each laugh I was further damning myself but having such a swell time I couldn't stop.

Mary, the most holy of all the saints. Virgin mother of Jesus. Heavenly assumption without death. La la la, and me laughing while Georgy lectured the statue on basic hygiene.

In the Middle Ages, lady chapels were built everywhere, including one shrine in England that claimed to have a vial of her breast milk. A cult like hers stirs up more rumors than legends about Lincoln. In recent times, Mary has popped up all over: Fatima. Lourdes. Guadalupe.

If you are a pitiful sinner and pray to her, she will intervene for you. Although I must be beyond pitiful. Hopeless, said Georgy, for this latest sign was a clear message. She was no longer safe to burn, so I unplugged her. Finally ended up stuffing her in a suitcase. Too afraid to throw her away.

The Baby Kicks

Life is starting to show more in Janey. She bought some maternity pants with elastic in the waist to match her white smock. "The baby's kicking," she says. "Do you want to feel?"

She takes my hand before I can answer. Lifts her smock and guides it to her warm belly. I want and don't want to pull away. Tha-thump, thump, thump. That baby is jogging in place. Or dancing, having a party of one. I keep my hand there for a while. Now I don't want to move. It's reassuring. The baby, Janey's hand on mine, the warmth of it all. She seems to know this and doesn't rush. I think I could fall asleep this way. Quietly and at peace. No bad dreams. Wouldn't it be nice.

"It's like a miracle, isn't it?" she says.

I close my eyes, feel the next kick, and imagine it to be Killian's baby. But Killian chased Janey away. To say that she married on the rebound is not really fair because I don't know the whole story about that trip to Hawaii. Except that she came back horribly hurt. So hurt her face was beyond hiding it.

I open my eyes. Smile at Janey. "That baby is going to be a runner for sure." Slowly I take my hand away. Warm and still feeling the throb of a hidden kick.

Janey looks at the crutches strewn on the floor. She picks them up, leans them against the wall. For a minute I think she's going to say something. Instead, she backs herself into a chair. "It's good to have a moment to sit down," she says.

"Careful. The glass." I suddenly worry about stray shards, hope none have been left on the chair.

She waves her hand dismissively.

"I don't know, Janey. These days I want to break anything in sight."

"Well, since you seem to fancy the televisions, you should know that Sam has two sets in his office."

"I don't care if he owns the appliance store next door. I'm not walking down there."

"Meghan—"

"No Janey, forget it."

"Why not?"

"He's doing it on purpose. He's mad I'm not wearing the prosthesis, so he's going to make me walk all over creation in these crutches. Put me on carnival display. Well, he can just kiss my ass, because

I'm not even walking on those." I cross my arms and look at the ceiling.

"Oh, Meghan."

"No way, Janey. No way. No how."

Footgear

I used to name all my shoes. Fast names: Mercury. Lightning. Flying Finns. Next to the runner's mindset, the shoe is the most important thing. I had a pair of old Converse once. White high-tops. Dropped a tear when Rabbit Feet wore out and I had to part with them.

New shoes come with one kind of sole. But they develop a different kind once you own them. Wear them. Break them in. Finally, they wear out, and it's like losing a piece of yourself. Separating them from all the memories. All the living you did in those shoes. You look for another pair and move on. You have to. That is, if you're alive. I remember Pop Kelley's shoes lined up in his closet like soldiers waiting for marching orders. Then he died and they were carted off. To the Salvation Army along with his clothes. Grammy should have kept the leather laces to his work boots. That little string of memory.

Pop Kelley never bought me new shoes, but once he saw two barefoot kids downtown and took them into the store. They came running out with new sneakers.

Shopping for the right pair is a little like taking a multiple-choice test. You guess wrong a few times before you get the correct fit. A lot of times you pay for the brand name and the shoe isn't worth the dog doo you step in.

For long runs and on roads you need something that absorbs more shock. Shoes with waffle soles. And a cushioning midsole.

At St. Cats you were always trying out new shoes. Narrow Adidas. Nikes. Pumas. They'd split or rip or just wear out. New Balance was a no-frills shoe in the color department. It held up okay. Half those shoes I wouldn't have worn if I had to pay for them with my own money.

When I compete I wear the lightest shoes I can find. Shoes can make the critical difference. And I'm only running miles, not for my life. Those guys in Vietnam, they really needed some kind of special footgear. Heavy leather was standard issue at the beginning. Waterlogged in no time. Wet stinking boots. Boots that rotted off in a couple of weeks. Even if they weighed a ton, wood splinters made from sharpened bamboo traveled right through them. Punji sticks. Hidden in tall grass or buried in pits, the tips coated in feces to guarantee infection. Then came jungle boots. Part boot. Part canvas sneaker. And Goodyear treads with hardy soles.

But no boot could keep socks dry. No boot could prevent jungle rot. Sores on the feet that never healed. Killian went through three pair in a year. And they were hard to come by. Especially on the front. Shoes with soul: the one thing that separated the seasoned soldiers from the cherries, the clerks, the supply sergeants.

Killian wrote the book on boots over there. Who would have thought brother and sister would have ended up experts in the same area while they were worlds apart.

Killian said to know how much a soldier had gone through, how much he could stand, he'd always look first at the guy's boots. Scuffed. Red-stained. Lacking polish. Those were boots to be proud of.

Postcard

Dear Mr. Lincoln,

What about your boots? Black. Size 14. Of this I'm sure. I know about the shoemaker's trick, too. How he put felt between your leather soles so they wouldn't squeak.

You blacked your own boots even as president. You know, Father Abraham, I would have shined your shoes. Rubbed the crackling leather with mink oil. Put my hand inside and felt the throb, the pulse, the stench, the wounds left by the chiropodist who operated on your feet. I believe I would have. Yes, I believe.

Your Thomasina,
Meghan

Lincoln and Legs

I have to know: What would Lincoln think about a girl with one leg?

Joke Legs

*I*f I could, I'd go back in time. Way back. Before Killian and his war. Before me. I'd walk downtown. Hop up the narrow stairs. To the second floor where Lincoln's law office was. Show my one-legged self to him. He'd be stretched out on the sofa. Reading the newspaper out loud in a way that always irritated his partner. I'd say, Mr. Lincoln, get a look at this. What do you think?

I bet he'd make a joke.

Maybe that wouldn't be so bad. Lincoln made jokes out of just about everything. If you can't laugh, you might as well choke on your tears and snot and get it over with.

Truth is, a new leg scares me. A mechanical graft. With a life of its own. Taking me places I don't want to go. Like the man's cork leg in the comic song Lincoln used to make a political point. Once it got going it wouldn't stop. And the more the man tried to make it stop, the more it ran away with him. But there's more. If the mechanical leg doesn't take off with me, then I'm afraid it'll fall off. Leave me just at the moment I need it the most.

Joke legs. When someone asked Lincoln how long a man's legs should be in proportion to his body, Lincoln said he figured that a man's legs ought to be long enough to reach from his body to the ground. Ha!

Still . . . uneven legs like mine would be a sorry thing to him. "What an awful thing it would have been," said Lincoln after his son was born, "if the child had been born with a long leg like mine and a short one like Mary's." Not as awful as having a matched pair and losing one. Never being able to forget what your two good legs used to be able to do. To be left with an itch you can never again scratch.

Maybe he would have liked me better with both legs. But maybe not. I don't know. He had a soft spot for misfits. Like his favorite son, Tad. Short for Tadpole, a nervous wiggler. He had crooked teeth and a messed-up palate. Screwed his speech all to hell. And at thirteen he still couldn't read. But Lincoln loved him best. And how kind he was to that little midget Tom Thumb and his wife. Bending down down down to shake their tiny hands.

Me and little Tadpole. Tom Thumb. All the other P.T. Barnum freaks. And Lincoln with his top-hat magic. Magic he made just by taking it off as the black troops marched by.

But the one thing I wonder about the most is not something he would have said so much as done. Early New Salem days. A wild group of boys challenged Lincoln. Wanted to see just how strong and quick he was. He won big-time. But he wasn't around the day that gang burned off the wooden leg of some old man. Holding him down until it all just burned off.

Would Lincoln have tried to stop them if he had been there? I know for sure he wouldn't have liked it. Any more than he liked slavery or cruelty to animals. But would he have done something about it? How could he not? Who could stand to watch that? Not him. No, not him. He wouldn't have let them add humiliation to the hurt that old man had already lived through.

Crutches

*P*J comes in, her nose all stopped up from the cold. "What are you working on, Meghan?"

"This Lincoln report."

She looks up to where the television used to be, a long black protruding arm. At the end, a square palm holding nothing. Hanging from the arm on a cord is the Rent-A-Leg. I've wrapped some twine around the foot and strung it up.

PJ sniffs and looks at all this without comment.

I stick my pencil in the book and close it. "TV blew a tube," I tell her.

From her book bag she takes a box of chocolate mint cookies. The last of the Girl Scout ones stashed in the freezer. Mint smell rises with the ripped cellophane. She puts the cookies in my lap, then reaches between my bed and nightstand and picks up the crutches.

"What are you doing, PJ?"

"Just playing around," she says.

"They're not toys."

"It's kinda fun." She's wobbling back and forth. They're too tall for her and she looks ridiculous. Wobble. Wobble. Everything about those damn crutches sets my hair on fire, but after a minute I can't help smiling. She's just too cute.

"Enjoy yourself." I bite into the cookie. Look at the green box. "I always wanted to be a Girl Scout," I tell PJ. "Get one of those pale green pocketknives with a bottle opener."

"Why didn't you?"

"I kept getting beat up in Brownies by a fat girl with long fingernails. She was always going for my face."

"So you quit."

"Yep. Now my favorite pastime is to look for her fat face on every box of Girl Scout cookies I eat."

PJ laughs and holds out the wide end of the crutch like a collection basket. "Cookie please."

She maneuvers the crutches away from me and I see her side profile. A shadow drawing from black construction paper like everyone gets in kindergarten. I shove another cookie in my mouth, chomping anxiously, wishing she'd sit down.

"You never wanted to fight her back, Meghan? You always fight everybody."

"I guess I figured you could always buy a pocketknife easier than a new face."

A few seconds later, poky little rubber steps, she shifts around to face me and plops into the chair. She rests the crutches underneath her legs, leaning them on the edge of the chair, her legs stretched out on top of them. "Meghan, these things . . . they're the funnest." She halts suddenly to sneeze. Cannon blast of crumbs.

When the black shrapnel lands on my hospital gown and white sheets I feel like laughing and crying all at once. "Then just take the damn things home with you, PJ."

"Jeez Meghan, you cuss all the time now. You used to tell me people cussed because their repertoire of adjectives was limited."

"Well, that was a lie. Now would you just put the goddamn crutches down for God sakes."

She starts to slide them under the bed, sees the shoe box and pulls it out. She lifts the lid and looks at the splendid shoes. "Are these what came from your friend?"

"Put those down, PJ!" I shout.

Her face starts to change. Her lower lip quivers. She's getting that look before she cries. She jumps up from the chair and grabs her coat. "I have to go now, Meghan."

"PJ. Wait."

She's out the door.

Damn. Damn. Dammit.

Climbing the Walls

I try to think about anything that has nothing to do with me. I reach for my little stack of post-cards, shuffle them through my fingers. One of the church where Mary used to drag Abe on Sundays. Another of his tomb. I look at the bricks and start laughing because they remind me of the time Georgy locked herself out of her room and climbed two stories up the red brick wall and through her window. All of the nuns were filing out of evening chapel and there was Georgy hanging up there like some apparition in baggy yellow pants and a white blouse. A couple of the older nuns who couldn't see too well fell to their knees and started praying.

That last part about the myopic nuns isn't quite true, but by the end of the evening that's how the story was being told. Georgy was on in-house suspension for two weeks. No phone calls. No room visitors. No weekend passes.

The hall monitor that month was Betsy Ballesteros. She would walk as fast as she could down the hall—running was against the rules—and knock on Sister Adele's door, to report on her hourly rounds.

Georgy and I had practically every class with Betsy. She'd sit in the front row and kiss every teacher's behind. Georgy said that Betsy spent so much time kissing rear ends that she couldn't recognize the faces they belonged to.

Having Betsy check up on her every hour of the evening was getting to Georgy. And every class with her, without a single break. One afternoon in English class when we were discussing "The Jilting of Granny Weatherall," Betsy starts rambling on about the secondary meaning of the story. She's talking about Christ as the bridegroom and junk like that. Well, Sister Roseanne starts getting real excited and little white spitballs are forming in the corners of her lips. You can tell she's impressed as hell with Betsy.

Betsy grins and asks Sister Roseanne if she thinks religious symbolism in the works of Katherine Anne Porter would make a good term paper. By then the little spitballs of excitement are the size of balloons and Sister has to stop to wipe them away. Georgy raises her hand and says, "Excuse me, Sister, but isn't

Katherine Anne Porter about the biggest living liar there is? Next to Nixon, I mean."

Betsy just froze, her face all stiff. In one sentence Georgy had cut her topic to shreds. Plus, everyone knew that Betsy's dad was on the Republican re-election committee. Betsy with her Nixon/Agnew '72 pin on her duffle coat.

The room got so quiet and tense that I jerked in my chair. I reached down and rubbed the bruise on my leg.

Sister Roseanne's smile was dropping faster than a clay load of bricks. Her skin color had just reached the ashen stage when the bell rang.

Sunk

*T*he last Friday of Georgy's in-dorm suspension she fled her room. She just couldn't take being cooped up any longer. A couple of nights she had managed to get a library pass and there every hour on the hour came Betsy, making sure she sat at the table alone. Most monitors would cut you some slack, but this was personal. Betsy broke her weekend dates just to be there every hour. It was costing her plenty, but she didn't care. She turned herself into her own religious symbol: thorn in Georgy's side.

When Betsy left the library, I came out of the stacks with my books and sat across from Georgy. We'd pass notes back and forth for the next hour. Georgy wrote in bold capital letters. Nothing mousy about her at all. When she showed up at the pool on the last day of her two-week torture, I knew the final battle lines were being drawn.

Three times a week during the off-season I'd swim there, breathing the warm chlorinated air in a pool the size of Texas. Laps right after biology class. That time of day it was deserted, especially on Friday. Everyone was changing out of uniforms, making phone calls. Getting ready for dinner. I had finished a lap of butterflies before I noticed her sitting on my towel. Her feet in the water. Jeans and shirtsleeves rolled up.

Behind her was a trail beginning at the door and leading into the steamy pool. Gloves. Scarf. Coat. Shoes. Socks. Seeing her, I smiled. I swam over to her, pushed up my goggles. My forearms on the edge of the pool, I rested my chin in between, letting my legs flip back and forth behind me.

"Some bruise you got there." She stretches and points with her toe in the water, touching the dark spot. I wince. Mostly because I expect it to hurt, though it doesn't.

"Couple of days now," I say. "From the weights on the Universal gym I guess."

"That must be sore."

"Not really."

"That's odd."

"Yeah, I guess."

Georgy tells me about a climb two summers ago. Loose rock slid away under her feet, bruising and cutting her legs all up.

A moment passes. She sees me staring at the tattoo on the inside of her forearm: an eagle with wings feathered back so far they almost meet on the front of the arm. The only tattoos I had seen before were indistinct blobs plastered on the biceps of sailors and cyclists who make up part of the annual state fair crowd. But Georgy's body art is nothing like theirs. It's blue and clear. I trace it with my finger. Georgy asks me if I like it and I tell her yes.

"We can get you one just like it this summer."

"That'd be great." I never thought about getting a tattoo myself, but just then the idea appeals to me. Not an eagle though. A winged helmet like Mercury's, maybe. On the back of my shoulder blade near my smallpox vaccination.

She pulls her arm back slowly and rolls down her sleeve.

"Let's go," she says, buttoning the cuff.

"Hey, wait a minute. This is your last day of suspension. Why are you doing this?"

"Because I can."

"What does that mean?"

But it was too late for an answer. I fell back into the water when I saw Betsy Ballesteros in the doorway, one hand on her hip. She'd caught Georgy this time and now the punishment would be doubled. A month of suspension and restrictions.

Georgy would never make it.

The Running Dream

*I*n the running dream there is no sound. I run in slow motion. The left leg back and the right rising. The knee comes high—past the waist and toward the chest—then begins to stretch itself forward. And I leave the ground in this high hurdle stride, as though there were no gravity. It is 1969 and I know what little pull there is on the moon and how incredibly far I can jump in just sweat clothes and cleated shoes. I am moving through the air. The arc of a gazelle with flowing full strides. Then I begin to hear a noise. The sound of blood pumping in my ears. I am aware. Of exhilaration. Of fear. Each time I leap a little higher. Glide a little farther. I sense—and then know for certain—that I could leave the earth all together and take flight. Chrysalis popping. My legs having become wings. But I am too afraid to fly, and always I wake when I am too high and am tumbling back to earth. Breathless. A damp ring of sweat around my hairline.

I bolt up. Open my eyes. See where I am. The shoes. I want the shoes. I lean over toward the night table, open the drawer. Grab the box of running shoes, squeeze it to my chest like a teddy bear. I open the box and the smell of rich leather makes me cry. For things that are. For things that can never be. I feel the tears slip over my hands and onto the shoes. Now they're baptized. But how can I name them? To name them at all is to change things forever in my mind, for I can never again give my shoes fast names. And I will lose my dream. My beautiful running dream, without ever having taken flight.

The Chicken Bone Case of 1856

A man broke both legs when a chimney fell on him. Doctors set his legs but the right one turned out crooked and shorter than the left. He sued. Lincoln defended the two doctors. Hard to believe, but he did. Said the elderly man was lucky to walk at all because old folks' bones are brittle. Less likely to mend. To prove his point, Lincoln used young and old chicken bones. Eventually the parties settled out of court. Abe must have needed vittles money to take that case.

More famous is the broken leg of John Wilkes Booth. Got a fractured tibia when he jumped onto the stage after assassinating Lincoln. Doctor Mudd set his leg. Spent years in prison for it.

I wonder what Lincoln would think of my doctor list. Of Doctors Take More and Take Less, for example. One thing's for sure. They would not laugh at his jokes.

Dear Mr. Lincoln,

Here is one for you: A woman goes into the hospital to have a bad leg removed. By mistake the surgeon cuts off the good leg. (God knows what they did with it.) Anyway, once the error was discovered, it was too late to reattach it. So they take her back into surgery. This time they cut off the bad leg. She sues. A clear case of malpractice and she loses. The judge said she didn't have a leg to stand on.

Ha! Bet your bones are clattering over that one.

Your Joker,
Meghan

Lincoln's Own Legs

Just how long were they? I'd like to have stood side by side and compared. Tied our two legs together. We could have run a three-legged race. Even with two legs, I'd look like a midget next to him. Lincoln was six feet four inches. But when he was sitting down, he looked the height of an average man. Except for his knees, which pointed up to the ceiling. He had this habit. After he told a good story, he'd wrap his arms around his knees, pull them up to his chin, and rock. Back and forth. All rounded and folded over, like those gray roly-poly bugs you find in the summer under cool rocks. What I'd give to hear one of those stories right now: My Jesus starter pack. The arrowhead Mr. Jacobs' plow turned up. One of my best letters from Killian. What I wouldn't give for a laugh lasting longer than one of his long legs.

A client once saw Lincoln's leg propped up on an office desk. Said that it was the longest he'd ever seen. So Lincoln pulled up his other leg. "Here's another one just like it," he said. But how long is long?

His law partner in Illinois traveled the circuit with him and was sure surprised to see those feet sticking way out into the room one night when they had to share a bed.

Wished I could have seen his big feet hanging out like he was some Kentucky hillbilly. Makes me start to giggle just thinking of it. Lincoln always used to say he wasn't much to look at. Newspapers agreed. Always describing him as kind of grotesque. But what a genius to listen to. They agreed on that, too. The best stump speaker. Stump.

Dear Mr. Lincoln,

All your life you saw maimed and missing legs. Did it ever disgust you? As a youngster, there were old veterans of the Revolutionary War. Later on, the War of 1812. Then the Civil War. Some drifted across the prairie into your practice. I read about the one-legged Mexican War veteran you defended, even though he was guilty.

Now my body is at war with itself. I

wonder what advice you might have for me. Would you give me the old leg divided against itself speech? The cancer is whacked off. Reconstruction begins. That sort of thing? Or would I become another one of your stories. The one-legged runner. The good-bye girl. The effete athlete.

Maybe you would teach me to laugh. Or to just get busy working and forget it. Some of both I guess. Truth is my legs are chicken bones through and through. Doesn't matter if they're young or old.

Your yellow-bellied friend,
Meghan H.

Wires Crossed

Janey says, "I brought you some more postcards. I hope you like them."

"Thanks." I take the paper sack.

"Do you need stamps?"

"No, that's okay."

"But how are you going to mail them without stamps?"

How to explain that? "I've got all the stamps I need," is all I answer. I set the bag down and pick up the game box and shake it. "Should I set it up?"

Back straight, Janey lowers herself into the chair by my bed. The extra weight is finally getting to her. There's a pained expression on her face.

"The baby?"

She looks down, and rubs one thumb with the other. Back and forth. "Your doctor," she says.

I knew it. Doctor Take More. After my other

limbs. My vital organs. My gray matter. I knew I should have refused that last blood test. Now PJ will get my big bedroom with the open view, spread her junk everywhere. "The hell with all doctors."

"Do you want to know what he said?"

Like I don't already. I go on imagining the worst things until she says Sam's name. Whoa. I put on the Flintstones brakes.

Wait a minute here. "Sam?" I listen like I hadn't before. No more Scrabble or special visits from Janey unless I do my physical therapy. Wear my Rent-A-Leg like a good little gimp.

"He says it's the best thing I can do right now to really help you, Meghan."

I want to throw all those wooden letters across the room. Janey. Janey my what? Almost sister-in-law? Nurse? Friend? Confidant? It's the worst kind of bribery. "So he's recruited you now too," I say lamely.

"You make it sound like some kind of battle, Meghan. We're all on your side, not against you."

The other shoe has finally dropped. He warned me he was going to do this. Said I was getting too comfortable with my room and routine, but I didn't believe him. And I didn't believe Janey would go along with it.

My mind is racing a million miles an hour and I slow it down trying to digest all this.

Mother of All Catfish

When Janey leaves, I pull the covers up tight around my neck and remember better times. I have to. Summer of '66. Killian would put PJ on the back of his banana seat, and we'd pedal out to Grass Lake. I rode behind them, watching the brim of PJ's hat flop up and down over the dirt roads. PJ had taken to wearing a straw hat and plastic pink sunglasses with lenses so dark you couldn't see her eyes. She was so sensitive to the rays. A real crispy critter if she stayed outside unprotected. But she'd pitch a fit if you tried to keep her out of the afternoon sun. Finally she agreed to the hat and sunglasses. She looked ridiculously sweet, like old ladies in lime green short outfits. Much as I wanted to, I never had the heart to make fun of her.

Grass Lake was about three miles away, past the Jacobs farm. Some folks would consider it a pond, but it was much bigger than the watering holes you see in grazing pastures. You had to cut through two fields and a big strawberry patch, then a clump of trees. Right behind them, the lake, hiding out. It used to be a well-kept secret and I liked to imagine we were the only ones who knew about it, but there was always a beer can or two around.

We'd go almost every afternoon when Killian wasn't working. He was sixteen then and shelved books at the library three days a week.

Looking back on that summer, it seems mostly perfect. Golden in the sun and green all around. It's gone now. But I remember it like yesterday. PJ unfolding her towel, curling up with her abacus. Me, flipping through *Mad* magazine, working my way to the famous last page.

One day we were lying there soaking up the sun when Killian shouted, "Fish! Big fish!" Then he stood over us, dripping water on my magazine, and told us he had found a huge catfish. So fat it couldn't move, just lay there sucking scum.

We all swam out to the deepest part of the lake. So deep the sunlight didn't reach the bottom. Didn't even come close. PJ in a dime-store inner tube treaded water on the surface, waiting. I followed Killian down, through the sun-green to gray-green to black water. My air gave out and I had to come up. Or maybe I was just scared. I tried again but my ears got to popping and my chest felt like it was folding in two. Even Killian was breathless. "Did you see it that time?" he gasped. I was too air hungry to answer. I had seen a murky mass, but I hadn't been close enough to really get a good look. Killian insisted he'd had it by its mossy tail. That it was over six feet long, five hundred pounds easy.

"You lie," I said. He was always trying to pull my leg.

"See for yourself." He smiled, his little teeth glinting like the water.

Later, I tried to find the spot but couldn't.

I turn on my side, punch the pillow a couple of times. Tomorrow I'll ask PJ if she remembers that summer at Grass Lake. Or maybe not. What if she remembers it differently? I spin this thought in my head like a 45 single. Over and over. The thought drags out to a slower speed: 33⅓. Slooooooow Painnnnnful . . .

Finally. I feel sleep coming. It's a funny unsure world in-between wake and dream. Floating in a haze of thought. Thinking about runners who can't run. Farmers who can't farm. Killian killing.

Falling Down

Sam looks at my crutches leaning against the wall, at my Rent-A-Leg hanging from the TV stand. He pokes at the leg with a finger and it sways back and forth like a gigantic bamboo chime. What sound does one hollow chime make in the wind? The same soundless howl as a one-legged runner.

"I pegged you all wrong, Meghan," says Sam. "I thought you'd be a fanatic for your new prosthesis. Thought you'd be up and running pronto."

"You were wrong to bet on this horse," I say. Prosthesis hell. I just got used to these goddamn crutches: puddle jump to the bathroom and back, to the candy machine in an emergency. Why drag a damn leg along as well? "You're just steamed because I never made it to your office. So what."

"No," he tells me, "that's not it at all." I've over accepted the whole thing, he says. He goes into a long-winded speech, and I yawn. I look down to see what Kool-Aid socks of the day he's wearing. Raspberry red. Lemon yellow. Orange orange.

"Do you understand what I'm saying?" he asks.

I grunt.

That hanging leg bothers the hell out of him. He cuts it loose with his pocketknife and leans it on the chair next to him when he sits down. It slides onto the floor like a stiff snake. We both watch. Then Sam reaches in his suit pocket and takes out a bottle of milk of magnesia. Shaking up MOM again. So funny, he thinks. Calling it MOM.

"So," I say, "you recruited Janey."

"Yes, I did."

I snort.

Sam asks me if I know about fishing, which of course I do, which of course he knows already, but he asks anyway. He goes on and on about fishing and hooking different kinds of fish and he ends up sort of telling me that I'm the biggest gar in this room. Bit a hook the size of his shoe. He talks about responsibility to ourselves and what we owe and don't owe to others. Eventually, somehow, it leads back to these crutches. Wouldn't it be better to walk without them some of the time? Why not wear a leg? "There really isn't any physical reason," he says, "why you can't walk."

Oh, sure. He talks about all the advances they're making with prosthetic devices and la la la. My luck

I'll end up with a plastic Ballesteros special. Glows in the dark. Seashells embedded in acrylic. The moving lawn ornament.

"I can't take any more today," I say.

"Same time same place tomorrow?" he asks.

"Whatever."

"Meghan," he says, "I'm sorry. Maybe I was wrong to ask you to come to my office." He says this like he feels pity for me and it sets my hair on fire.

I don't say anything back.

When he leaves, I lie in the quiet for long time, then lean forward and reach for the crutches. I pull myself up. Stand still and look around. At the sorry hobo on the dresser. At the crumpled sheets. At the leg on the floor. Leg. I stare at that sorry chunk of junk for a long time. I hobble over to it. I lean against the wall, a balancing technique I've already learned, then bend over and reach for it. I don't know why. Maybe just to look at it again, but I lose my balance and smack my face hard into the tiled floor. Soon blood is filling my mouth with a metallic taste.

Truth and Consequences

"Come on," said Georgy. She was pulling me hard by my wrist. I felt the burn of the pool's stone edge scrape against my thighs.

"What now?" I pictured Betsy in full gallop across the campus, her broken dates and sundry sacrifices all worth it.

"We'll retreat and form a plan of action."

I didn't look at Georgy. Ten minutes ago I had been happily swimming. Now I might as well be debris at the bottom of the pool. Or soon enough I would be. Trouble was cooking and I was in the pot. Mechanically I dried myself off with a towel.

Georgy put on her shoes and coat, leaving her socks and scarf and gloves. I ran after her, picking them up. "What about these?"

"Not important. Hurry up and change. They'll be coming with both barrels."

I knew what she meant. Barrel one: Sister Pauline, the dean of students. Barrel two: Sister Adele, the housing director. I stripped out of my Speedo and pulled on my sweats, dug my bare feet into Converse sneakers.

We ran back to the dorms, a whirl of snowflakes falling around us, my hair wet as a baby's diaper. Up two flights of stairs. Taking the steps by twos and threes. In the hall was old Betsy herself, pounding away on Sister Adele's door.

No answer. Hallelujah. For the moment we were safe.

Betsy turned to face us. "Just you wait," she said.

That got to Georgy. She stopped so quick in her tracks that her boots squealed. "Betsy," she said, "your price tag is showing. It says two cents. For two cents you'd sell out your own grandmother."

I tugged at Georgy's sleeve. With effort she unlocked her eyes from Betsy's. We ran into my room and bolted the door.

For a moment all I could think of was clearing out. Running away. I knew Georgy could never put up with the swarm of constraints headed her way, and I couldn't imagine life at St. Cats without her. Death by boredom. I picked up my toothbrush, then stared at the books on my desk and, like a fool, wondered if I should take my homework. A million things were buzzing in my head at once.

What a jar of bees. Suddenly I was pushing a dresser in front of the door.

"What are you doing?"

"Barricading us in," I said. "It's what they do in the movies."

"Yeah, well. That's not where the movie usually ends."

I turned around to face Georgy. "You're cooked, aren't you?"

"Toast."

The bees were really rattling in my brain. "Maybe not," I said. "Listen. It's her word against ours. Two against one. I could say you were never there." I'd never told that kind of lie before. Most of my lies had been the kind designed not to hurt other people's feelings.

"Are you kidding? Around here Betsy's got more brownie points than Betty Crocker."

Georgy didn't have a brownie factor. Cold and smart-mouthed, especially to Sister Adele, who would praise God for an opportunity like this.

Worry must have been scribbled across my face, thicker than doodles in the margin of my physics notes. Georgy crossed the room and slid down on the floor next to me.

"We could run away," she said. "Far, far away."

"To where?"

"Anywhere you want to go."

For a moment it seemed possible. We'd get work,

change our identities, live in the woods, or in a cave in the mountains. Then I thought about Killian silently wandering the midnight streets. And PJ. And running. It wasn't that easy.

I pushed myself up and went to the window. Snow was coming down softly. Big cottony flakes. I could see them float and twirl, caught in the distant headlights of rush-hour traffic. Below I watched the back of Betsy's camel-hair coat cutting a path across the quad, a straight shot toward the dean's office.

The Bell Tower

Georgy jumps up and pushes the dresser away from the door. "I've got an idea."

I watch Betsy disappear into the administration building then turn to face Georgy. "It better be snappy."

I follow her down the hall into her room. She's grabbing ropes and clips and junk like that off the wall. Like lightning I understand. There is no doubt in her mind—she isn't coming back. "Listen," she says, "I'm going for broke. I've always wanted to scale that bell tower. It's now or never."

Georgy grabs a small backpack—the canvas kind you get in an Army surplus store—and throws in the food on her shelf. A bag of Fritos. A package of Oreos. Two apples. Then she rushes over to her bed, unzips her pillow case, and pulls out a small bag of marijuana. She throws it on top with a box of matches and straps the bag shut. She puts on socks, climbing boots, and a turtleneck. I watch her make all these preparations—wanting to stop her, but not. Part of me thinks there is still a way out. But there isn't. And Banker be damned, I'm not going to stay trapped here either.

"I'm going too," I say.

"No," says Georgy. "Stay out of it. So far you haven't ruffled any feathers."

At first that stings. But then I realize she is only trying to protect me. Doesn't want to drag me into this mess.

"What could they do to me?" I ask.

I've never been in trouble before. At most they might throw me a suspension. I don't care. This is Georgy's last hurrah and I want in.

"I'm going," I say. "You can't stop me." I'm sure I can do it. Scaling the bell tower couldn't be that much different from climbing the quarry.

Georgy turns and looks at me. "Your hair's wet."

"I'll dry it."

The bells chime. Evening Mass is about to begin.

"Just hurry up."

I wave the dryer around my head and pull a stocking cap down almost to my eyes. A turtleneck, a wool sweater, and a down vest come next. I yank a baggy pair of jeans out of my drawer, pushing one leg in as I dance around the room on the other, looking for my shoes.

From there we beat it down the back stairs, across the courtyard to the chapel. Betsy storms back out of the building, waving her arms in frustration. Too flustered to even see us. Now she'll have at least an hour's wait. Even Betsy knows better than to interrupt praying nuns.

Behind us is the dorm, a checkerboard of yellow lights brightening up the snow. With these and the other lights, we can see clearly. I look up at the bell tower. A mile high in the sky. My heart is pounding. Scared and excited at the same moment.

Georgy tosses me a climbing belt and I put it on. She puts on a harness. Bundles of rope are at our feet. Speckled purple and orange. Aqua and yellow. Next thing I know she's messing with anchors and slings. Before it's all over with, she will use every feature on the building to get us to the top: window ledges, chinks in stone, old scaffolding anchors, even a flagpole.

She begins by hammering away between the mortar of the bricks and sticking in little metal gadgets, just like at the quarry. She adjusts the ropes, fiddles with these crampon things on her belt, pulls herself up and starts all over again.

About five feet off the ground, she turns and looks at me. "Okay now, you remember . . ." She goes over all the instructions like before.

"Alright," I say. Her words seem faint because blood is pumping in my ears. But the sound fades as

I begin climbing, following her moves. Everything seems smooth and liquid, almost like in a dream. I look down for a second and can hardly believe how far up I already am. My heart flutters. Above me I hear Georgy hammering softly and I pause.

Halfway up, the tips of my fingers feel icy. I position myself so I can blow on them. The skin is scraped raw. I blow again, warm hot breaths. Out of the corner of my eye, I see first one, then another shadow of a student in the window across the quad. My foot slips and I grab quickly with my hands. "They're watching us from the dorms," I say.

"Pay attention," says Georgy.

I hear a window open in the distance, the crackling ice on it breaking away followed by a whistle. Then a clap.

Another window cracks open. A familiar voice yells, "You're dead now."

I concentrate on what I'm doing. Check my footing and grip. We keep climbing. Georgy's near the top now and suddenly I want to look down again but don't. I wait until Georgy's safely over the parapet. Then she helps me over. It's like we're in a small gondola suspended in the air. Now, finally, I look down. "Holy shit!"

"It's great, isn't it?" says Georgy.

I can see far. Way down the highway. A ribbon of yellow light. And further off into town, the dome on the old state capitol glows a pleasant firefly orange.

Beyond that, patches of dark farmland stretch out like an ocean at night, followed by a sprinkling of lights in the distance. "Wow." Now the windows are really cracking open and girls are clapping and hooting. We wave to all of them below.

"There's high," says Georgy. "And there's higher." She takes off her backpack and opens it up. The metal tips of the straps clank on the cement floor of the tower. In half a minute the smoke of marijuana is spiraling out. A couple of times before, Georgy had smoked in front of me. I took a puff once, coughed and coughed. Now it's different. I don't care if I cough my heart out. Soon my eyes feel wide and my ears funny. My fingers tingle more than before. I blow on the tips of them.

My throat feels dry. Next thing I know I stick out my tongue and catch big flakes that are swirling around. I start laughing for no reason and Georgy laughs too. We're a couple of giggling fools up there in the bell tower.

She breaks open the cookies and we start pulling them apart, eating the center first and then the chocolate outside. We stop about halfway through the bag and start in on the Fritos.

"This is the best time in my whole life," I say.

"Oh shit!"

"What?"

"The bell." Georgy jumps up. She grabs one of her metal gizmos and fastens it to the clapper, then hitches it to a rope and ties it around the outside of the bell.

We would have been a couple of Helen Kellers if that big hunk of metal had taken to clanging. Which it would have any minute, to signal the end of Mass or the beginning of dinner—however you want to look at it.

I lean over the edge of the parapet and watch the side door of the chapel open, throwing a long patch of white light onto the glittering snow. Nuns the size of candy bars file out the door. Fifty or so girls are still clustered in the dorm windows, some with their noses pressed to the glass, others hanging out and hooting. Girls also stand in the quad, looking up at us instead of beating a path to the chow line. By now the Double Barrels and their black-and-white entourage are beginning to figure out something is amiss. Next I see a lone figure running across the quad from the dorms toward the chapel.

"Good old Betsy," I say. Making a beeline to the dean and housing director.

Georgy cups her hands to her mouth megaphone style and boos. All the candy bars below suddenly grow round white faces that stare up at us.

We laugh like two fools. Then Georgy taps me on the shoulder. "Look," she says.

I turn around. Georgy points to the bell swaying silently. No sound. It's suddenly the funniest thing

I've ever seen. A swinging bell with its clapper tied shut. Tears are streaming down my face.

Below, they're having a whole conversation, none of which I can hear, but I can pretty well guess. The dean's trying to figure out how we got up here, because the bell tower's always locked. Betsy doesn't waste her time on the dean. Instead, she's jabbering at Sister Adele, pointing to the evidence on the scaled wall.

By now every window in the place is wide open, and more students flock over to them, listening, waiting to see what will happen next.

"You girls come down right now!" The words seem to crack in the cold air.

"When the angels sing," yells Georgy.

"Open the bell tower door and come down those stairs immediately."

"You heard Sister Adele," calls Betsy.

"I've had about all I can take of her," says Georgy. She grabs a cookie and lets it fly at Betsy.

An Oreo whizzing from the bell tower. That's how it all started. Next thing we're both dropping them like rocks in a Neanderthal skirmish. Black robes flying in all directions. And all the spectators hooting and clapping. One of those chocolate sandwiches, we later find out, hit Sister Adele's glasses, which in turn cut her nose.

That's what did it. Hard to believe, but a cookie from that high up can be dangerous. Offed by an

Oreo. Mutilated by a Mallomar. There could be worse ways to go. I know that for sure. Still, that's what did it.

But I don't regret it. Not one crumb.

Morning

Five stitches in my lip. What a jolly circus my life has become. My lip feels huge, like it might split all over again if I try to talk. I drink the orange juice on my breakfast tray, keep the straw away from the sore side of my mouth, but some of the citrus gets in the wound and stings. I drink it all anyway.

I have to get on the crutches again because if I don't, I know I never will. Let alone do what I have to do next. Slowly I move into the bathroom. On a hook is my red-and-black checked robe. Underneath, propped up at a crazy angle, is the Rent-A-Leg.

I lean against the wall, grab my bathrobe, and carry it back into the bedroom, holding it between my teeth. I sit on the edge of the bed to put it on, my trusty crutches on either side of me. I pull on an Acorn slipper and push myself up.

Slowly I move. Out the door into the hallway of everyone else's world. With my nose, I push the elevator button.

A candy striper my age gets on the elevator. She smiles at me with sympathy. I'd like to crank her with a crutch.

The door opens. It's a long hallway leading to Sam's office. Damn crutches. My armpits are starting to hurt. My lip hurts. My leg hurts. Every damn thing hurts, even what's not there.

The office is wide open. Guess they phoned I was on my way up. No secrets in this place. Hell, they probably count your sheets of toilet paper.

Sam stands in the doorway and smiles. He's caught in a huge rectangle of morning light coming from his office window. "Glad to see you."

He stands to the side and lets me pass. His office looks like PJ's room. A disaster area. But the floor's clear. That's all I care about.

Sam points to an easy-access chair. "Didn't bring your water pitcher, Meghan?"

"I travel light on first dates."

"How do you feel?"

"Like cow shit on a rainy day." I ease into the chair. Stacks of journals are piled along the wall and on his desk. I lift a crutch and point to the nearest stack. "You read all this junk?"

"Naw. Just the table of contents. Then if anything sounds interesting I read it."

We sit in silence for a moment as I try to imagine what exciting thing could be lurking behind the dull green covers.

"It took guts, you traveling down here today."

Surprised, I look up at Sam. "Guts?"

"What would you call it?"

I shake my head, at a loss for words. After Sam got through with me, and I found myself nose down on the floor, I felt like I was lying in my own caca. It was either get myself back on my foot or die from my own stink. "Scared. I'd call it scared."

It's a struggle to explain it to Sam. I'm not sure I understand it myself. How I've been lying there doing nothing, and now suddenly, the nothing fills me with panic. "You wound my clock yesterday. I could hardly see straight, I was so mad. And then when I fell . . . well, that made it even worse."

"Sometimes a person has to hit bottom before they can begin the long climb out," Sam says.

"Jeez you're good with clichés." But still his words make me want to cry. I touch my lip. "Think there'll be much of a scar?"

"Best plastics man around was on call. Lucky for you."

"That's exactly what he said, too." The mutual admiration society of white coats.

"You know, Meghan." Sam pauses. "You can do this. You can walk again."

"You sound like an advertisement for Lourdes.

Just hang your crutches by the water and walk away."

He laughs.

"Did you ever wonder why we've got no modern-day saints?" I ask him. "Why it's all become plastic replicas, dashboard Jesuses and glow-in-the-dark rosaries that come in the mail from missionaries begging donations?"

Now he doesn't say a thing and suddenly I remember. "I guess you wouldn't know about that stuff."

Sam smirks. "I do have a Christian friend or two."

"Well I think it's kind of sad. Like autumn."

He nods.

After a while, we come back to the leg.

I think about the pinkish plastic tube leaning against my bathroom wall. For the first time I wonder if Rent-A-Legs come in other colors. Mix and match.

"Christ," I say to Sam, "I fall down just trying to put the damn thing on. Can't imagine what fun awaits once it's chummed up to my leg."

"It's just temporary, Meghan. Don't lose sight of that."

"It's big and clumsy and I hate it."

"Temporary, Meghan. Temporary."

"As in the good one will be arriving shortly."

"Exactly."

"There is no good one."

We sit for a while not talking. The only sound is

from Sam's pencil as he taps it against his teeth.

By the time I leave his office I'm tired. Really tired. Boneless tired. I want a miracle. I want Killian. Or Honest Abe. He could pick me up and tuck me under one arm. I stop for a minute to catch my breath and give my arms a rest. The hallway is empty, and I know that's the way it will stay. Miracles went out when plastic saints came in.

Dear Mr. Lincoln,

What did you believe? Were you a scoffer at Christianity like some people claimed? It's easier not to be. Like McDonald's, millions and millions sold. Sorry. I forgot those weren't around in your day. I laugh at little icons. But I love them too. I had a plastic Mary at school for a while. But now she's buried in a Samsonite coffin on my closet shelf. Mostly my scoffing is quiet and comes late in the night when I lie awake and know—I just know. There's no damn sense to anything beyond our best efforts. Oh, Mr. Lincoln, I have put my finger into the wound and still I do not believe.

Your doubting Thomasina,
Meghan Hartman

Stopping the Bullet

Lincoln once sent a Massachusetts soldier a new Bible. The old one the soldier had carried in his breast pocket. Until it stopped a rifle ball.

In Vietnam it was shrapnel through a GI's helmet. Stopped short of the temple by a hunk of hashish wrapped in a Baggie. On more than one occasion, bullets whizzed by Lincoln's head too. His stovepipe hat was shot clean through while he was wearing it. But the sniper was never to be found. Like the enemy in Vietnam.

Landing

The letter was sticky with his fingerprints. Heat. So hot you think you are in hell. And the stench of everything rotting and burning around you. That's what Killian wrote about when he landed. Excrement. Napalm. Diesel fuel. Decomposing vegetation.

It seemed odd next to his descriptions of swimming pools and movie theaters. Lots of places to eat. I was trying to put together a picture of two different worlds.

For some reason this thing I had read about Salvador Dali stuck in my brain. Dressed in a diving suit, he went to give a lecture. He climbed out of a fancy car—in his mask and flippers—and heads and heads of cauliflower fell out with him.

Three days later, Killian and some other cherries packed their duffel bags and set out for a place called Cu Chi.

Cu Chi

*C*herries. The nicest thing they called new soldiers. FNG. Fucking New Guy. That too. Cu Chi was full of FNGs who stood in yet more lines to be further processed: Ground chuck. Sirloin. Rump roast.

They were fenced in by strands and strands of concertina wire. Mines. Booby traps. Killian said not to worry because it was very safe and big. There was talk of sapper attacks, where a VC would come up out of the ground. They had tunneled all under that place like ants. But most of that was old stories. Tunnels into the perimeter in the early days.

Killian didn't see Charlie or sappers or gooks the whole time he was at Cu Chi. But Charlie was out there. You could bet on it. Bet on it.

Killian believed everything he had been told stateside. Everything in advanced training. Once in

Vietnam he expected to run off the plane dodging bullets. But it wasn't like that at all. If you took away the heat and the smells it was almost like Anywhere, U.S.A.

Cu Chi was big too. Here they issued him field equipment and he had another week of training before he entered the field. Everyone was telling him to forget what he learned in the States. That was then. This is now.

Freezer Burns

*I*n bed, I feel where my leg was. Move my hand slowly up my thigh, across my chest and touch my torn lip. I am coming apart at the seams. Where is the glue to stop this unraveling? Will it stop? Will I be around long enough for all this to become a terrible memory? The kind that is so bad that just thinking of it leaves my chest frozen solid. I grab my pillow and prop myself up. I can't breathe. I picture the alveoli at the end of my lungs: tiny heads of cauliflower that have been left in the freezer too long. Little ice hairs form on the end. Sam calls these moments panic attacks. I call them freezer burns.

I start adding up the sub-zero moments. I crack with cold when I think of the photo I stumbled on by accident while Killian was in Vietnam. I was taking out the garbage after dinner and the bag broke. In between limp spinach and a ground-beef package was a torn-up letter and photograph from Killian. I picked out the pieces, separating them from the garbage. This was strange because we always left Killian's latest letter under a refrigerator magnet, until everyone had read it. When a new letter would come, we would put the old one in a drawer with the others. Saved them all. So what was the meaning of this?

I spread the jigsaw out on the floor of my room, starting with the photograph, which had been torn in four equal pieces. I taped them with Scotch tape. A man lying on the ground emerged. A dead man.

In the first quadrant was a hand reaching toward green foliage. I followed the arm over to the second section—a head and a shoulder with no face. Below the outstretched arm were legs, sort of pulled up and tucked in like a bad stomachache position. There was nothing but dirt in the last square of the picture.

It took a while longer to piece the letter together but I learned that the dead man in pajama clothing was Killian's first confirmed kill. He sent the picture like he was proud of it, like a cat that leaves robin entrails on the doormat.

I hid the evidence in my cigar box. The tape all yellow and crinkly now. Me, the keeper of the pieces. Even when I looked at the whole ragged puzzle, I still couldn't really see it. The picture didn't freezer burn me until I was lying in bed that night. Thinking about it. Then I jumped out of bed. Turned on the light. I reached underneath the bed for the cigar box and took out the picture. There was no gun.

That faceless soldier in the picture never had a gun.

Postcard

Dear Mr. Lincoln,

Could you pick up a gun and shoot a man? Hunt a human? Would you do it to save the Union? There was no Union to save in Vietnam. I think if it meant my life I could do it. Otherwise, the space grows larger between me and my brother. A gap so large. Now tell me. How do you cross a chasm that is too deep and wide for even a bridge? You left only a few clues before you died about how to reunite those who had once been so close. I am scratching around for those clues in the dirt.

Hey, do I look like a detective to you?

Your friend,

Nancy Drew (alias Meghan Hartman)

Firing Words

We are killing each other with words, firing them from our mouths. Short staccatos. Long angry blasts. The whole hospital can hear. Janey's come and gone. Ducked a crutch aimed at the Banker.

He's got the bill tightly clenched in his hand. "I'm telling you I'll be damned if I'm paying for another television set."

I don't answer.

"Do you hear me?"

"So don't pay."

He lets out a long sigh through his teeth. "What has gotten into you? You're breaking televisions, dragging me out of meetings over mice. Is that doctor doing you any good at all?"

"Leave Sam out of it," I say.

Next he starts in on St. Cats. The expulsion. The cookie assault. Blah. Blah. Blah.

"Hey," I say, "I never wanted to go there in the first place."

"Half the time you don't know what's in your own best interest, Meghan."

"You don't always know what's best either."

He looks down at his shiny shoes. He stares at them so long I wonder if he sees his reflection. Or maybe he's just counting the tiles on the floor. "Most of the time I do. Most of the time I do a pretty good job, but you don't want to see that part." Finally he looks up.

I snort at that one. "Yeah, like you knew what was best for Killian."

"Don't you dig there," he says. "You don't know anything about it."

That comment stings my eyes but I'm not giving him the satisfaction of seeing it firsthand. "Killian's wrecked," I shout. "And here I am hobbling behind him. You're doing a swell job. Just steer clear of PJ." Arrow to the heart.

"How dare you," he says.

"How dare I? How dare I?" I shout back, wishing for a fast smart line that won't come. Something to make him lose his grip.

"Never," he says, his blue eyes narrowing, "talk to me that way again. Not while you live in my house. Under my roof."

"Fine. You own everything. The roof. The house. The car. Half the farms in the county, but not me.

You don't own me. I do what I want."

"And that has gotten you real far, hasn't it?"

I roll my eyes. "Here we go again."

"You're damn well right," he says. "You had the perfect opportunity and you threw it away. You've got a good brain. St. Catherine's would have pushed you to use it more, but you had to go play rebel."

My survival odds are good. I'm fair game this week. "Just go ahead," I say. "Feel free to roll out the whole cookie cutting adventure."

The dean could have lived with the marijuana and the chapel climbing, but to have undermined Sister Adele's authority in front of all those girls and then—assault her with a cookie. That, she couldn't live with.

"You're just like your grandfather," he says, "willing to risk everything for a whim. What in God's name were you thinking?"

Once again he's buried me in the graveyard of his disappointment. Lumped me right in there with all the others. "Aces to royal flush isn't a whim. I would have made that bet too."

"Don't get smart."

"Me? Smart? Didn't you just say that's why you sent me to that hellhole in the first place?"

"Listen, Meghan. I had no idea you hated St. Catherine's that much."

Whoa. I stew on that one for a second. But then I

get madder. "How could you know. You never ask. You never listen."

"There's no school that teaches you how to be a father," he says.

"If there was, you'd have to repeat the year and go to summer school."

Bingo. His face goes red and he tugs at the knot of his tie. He's still holding it together, but I can feel the heat from across the room. Hear the air through his teeth again, fast and whistley like a steam kettle about to flip its top.

"There's no talking to you," he says.

He turns and points to the empty arm of the television set. I know he's trying to catch his breath.

"Your behavior, young lady, has escalated unchecked. And it's going to stop right now, beginning with that so-called doctor."

"I fire my doctors, not you," I shout. "And Sam stays."

"Not while I'm paying the bills." Not. Not. Not.

I let fly another crutch in his direction. For sure he'll hit me now. Even though he never has before, I can see it in his eyes as he comes toward me—all the icy anger mirrored right back at me.

There's a bang as Sam flies through the door, pushing it so hard it smacks against the wall.

"Back off," he shouts. "Now."

The Banker turns to face him. Blue suit. White shirt. Red, red face. Anger has silenced him beyond words. Or maybe he has just begun to regain his composure. In his right hand I hear a crunching sound. Wadding the bill into a tight ball. He drops it on the floor. "You." He points at Sam. "You're fired."

IV.
Husking

Just When . . .

"How can he do that, Janey?" Half an hour later and the veins in my neck are still throbbing.

"Give him some time to cool down, Meghan."

"He can cool off in hell." Just like that. Fired. He might as well have knocked the crutches out from under me. Nailed a foreclosure sign across my chest. But then, that's what bankers do. That's how they stay in business. I imagine the days ahead without even a glimpse of Sam's mismatched socks, but I'm too mad to cry.

Janey takes my hand, squeezes the fingertips. I watch the nail beds turn red. Red is all I see.

"Whatever happens," she says, "you'll get through it."

I half smile, wondering if she said the same thing to Killian before he left for Vietnam. He got through the nightmare alright, and now the nightmare is in him. And no one can help him.

Ears and Cornfields

1) Ears. When I was a kid, I watched this *Twilight Zone* episode on TV where some deadly bug crawled into a man's ear. He was a goner for sure. Miraculously, he managed to get the bug out, only to find it had laid its eggs inside him.

That's what I think about Killian. He made the great escape from Vietnam, but it laid eggs in his head that keep hatching tiny horrors.

I think about the two guys on his squad. His best friend, Snoopy, had huge ears. Creeper just collected them. Around his neck on a chain. Sick as it sounds, it's not a new horror.

During the Civil War, Harriet Beecher Stowe got a package in the mail. All the way up to Maine came a pair of negro ears. Minus the negro. Just as bad, a Southern terrorist used to fill the ears of Union soldiers with gunpowder and blow their heads off.

Then collect the ears. What there was left to collect, I can't quite figure. Lincoln—who could find mercy for most—had none for that ear collector.

2) Cornfields. The governor of Iowa was working in his cornfield when a telegram arrived from President Lincoln asking him to raise a regiment of militia for the Union. Not long after, at the battle of Antietam thousands of soldiers fertilized another cornfield with their blood. Closer than fallen stalks lay their bodies. War in a cornfield. Corn stripped of its ears, men stripped of their lives. How much sense does that make?

Postcard

Dear Mr. Lincoln,

    The Spanish-American War. The War to End All Wars. World War II. The Korean War. The Vietnam War. We have been busy since you left us. Soon I think we will do it just to do it. The reasons become as green as money—or maybe just grayer—all the time.

                  Sincerely tired of it,
                  Meghan Hartman

P.S. Did I mention the Meghan-Banker Wars?

Doorway

It's after dinner, dark. Visiting hours are over. I lock myself in the bathroom, lean my crutches against the wall. I sit on the edge of the tub. It's cold even through my bathrobe. I push my good foot forward on the floor, test the traction of my sneaker. It's A-okay. Just don't let me fall and break my one good leg.

I close my eyes, try to prepare myself mentally. Visualization. I used to do it before each race. Now the stakes seem so much higher. I open my eyes, look down at the stump. It still scares the hell out of me. Meghan Hartman, covered in stumps like Mr. Potato Head, that plastic kid's game.

Visualize, dammit. At least the seam is good. Neat. I'll give Doctors Take More and Take Less that much credit.

I reach for the baby powder on the sink and

shake some into my left hand. It's soft. I push it around my palm with my finger before smoothing it onto my leg. The stump feels smaller. Looks smaller too. Still, the swelling seems to go on forever. But it's what's left of my leg now, and I'm keeping it.

Next to the towel is my stump sock. I unfold it and pull it on just like I used to do with knee socks. Now for the suprapatellar cuff. Big word for a garter belt that helps keep the leg in place.

In the corner by the door my Rent-A-Leg rests all by its lonesome. I think of some store mannequin missing a part, but the part is mine and I'm real, even though the leg isn't. I lean forward as far as I can until I can grab it by the ankle and pull it across the floor. I guide my stump into the socket. It's like putting on a shoe. That's how I try to think of it. I'm tightening the straps much like I would laces.

Now, I'm all together. Ha! I sit for a second longer. Exhale slowly. Then use my hands to push myself up off the tub's edge. Next, I grab hold of the towel rack. It wiggles and I panic; little black dots do a dance in front of my eyes. But I'm still standing. All the weight is on my left foot. Gradually I start to shift it to the right. Pressure from the plastic socket pushes against my stump. It isn't a sharp pain I begin to feel but more like a dull pressure, a sore ache. I slide a crutch beneath my arm. Breathe again slowly. Ready. I unlock the door, poke the crutch out first, and tense my thigh muscles to lift the weight of

Rent-A-Leg. I expect it to fall off any second, but it pushes out in front of me just like it's supposed to. Two more steps. Same thing.

I stop in front of my door, stand with my weight on both feet. Stand on both feet. I can't believe it.

I make my way down the hall slowly, staying close to the wall. Me, Rent-A-Leg, and one crutch. I look down at the Rent-A-Leg. Better than empty space between my knee and the floor. At least so far. And this way he'll see I'm serious. He'll take me back. He'll have to.

Blue TV-screen light filters through the blackness of half-opened doors. When I get on the elevator, a nurse from another floor is already there, leaning her bulky self against the handrail. She looks at her watch. "You're not supposed to be off your floor at this hour."

What is she, the grown-up version of a hall monitor? "I'm sleepwalking. It helps me to relax."

She starts to say something else, but I'm already at my stop.

On Sam's floor, the lights are turned way down because it's mostly daytime offices in this wing. Maybe he won't be there and I can forget all about it. I've never begged for anything. But I picture myself suddenly down on my good knee, like a child before a statue on a holy card. Please be my doctor, I pray. I'll pay you back if I live long enough to get a job.

A sliver of yellow light rims the bottom of his office door. I stop in front of the door and stare at it for a long time. A little bit of the light covers the tip of my terminal device. That's what I have now instead of a right foot.

I know I couldn't have gotten this far without Sam. Halfway up the mountain and the Banker cuts the rope. I lean the crutch against the wall, out of sight, and knock on his door. Wait for him to say come in, but he doesn't.

I hear a shuffling of papers and I knock again. Wait. Wait. Finally. Sam's hair is standing at crazy angles from his head, making me think of a cartoon cat, electrified.

"Meghan."

"Aren't you going to at least invite me in for a farewell drink?"

"I'd like to but I can't."

"You mean you won't." I feel like Rent-A-Leg is melting away from under me. I grab the door frame.

"Meghan, I'm in a tough spot here. Give me a couple of days to try to work things out. I'm sure I can work it out."

"But look," I say, "I'm wearing the damn leg."

"Meghan."

What a brush-off. Used to beg me to come to his office, now he won't let me past the door. "Forget you. You're just like everyone else. I should have known." It will be all right, promised Doctors Take

More and Take Less. You'll be able to run again, promised the Stupid Leg Man. The cancer is gone, say all the rest.

I grab my crutch and leave him standing in the doorway.

A Double Whammy

Dear Mr. Lincoln,

I am sorry to pester you again so soon but the truth is I am so scared that I don't know what else to do. Maybe I should pray to God? Did you ever? I know when your boys Eddie and Willie died you thought a lot more about the subject. And after Gettysburg too. Your wife described your religion as a kind of poetry in your nature. I think I understand that. When my mom died all the flowers seemed to make it worse. I never told anyone this before, but after her funeral I went to the hardware store and bought a dozen live crickets. I took them to a grassy field and let

them all go. It was the only thing that
made me feel the least bit better.

.   .   .

cont.

Do you think I should turn some crickets
loose for my leg? Do you think it's time
to turn some loose for Killian too? I
hope not. Am I asking too many questions? It's just that the Banker has
fired my doctor and I don't have anyone to talk to. I probably deserved it
because I have been yelling and tearing
up a lot of stuff lately. Since my mom
died my dad has gotten a lot stricter,
maybe because he has to decide everything by himself now. The truth is I don't
even know anymore why I'm so mad at
him, except about Killian. Everything else
is gray ground. I am so tired now and
it's cold in here tonight. Good night, Mr.
Lincoln. I hope I dream about the poetry
in crickets.

Sincerely,
Meghan Hartman

Shades of Gray

1) The Asian country of Thailand was known as Siam in 1861. That year the king of Siam offered President Lincoln elephants. Dozens of them. But Lincoln said, "No, thank you."

2) In Vietnam, there was elephant grass. Its density covered the jungle. Its sharp edges cut the soldiers. You could hide behind it in an ambush. And it would take all your strength to break a trail through it.

3) Civil War soldiers who had known combat called it "seeing the elephant."

4) In Vietnam you hardly ever saw the enemy face to face. Often on night patrol you held on to the back of the guy ahead of you. Your arm a proboscis, grabbing the shirttail in front of you. Hoping

you don't get lost. Hoping you don't step on a mine.

5) Losing Sam is like stepping on a mine. My gray matter is splattered all over the place.

6) If you do step on a mine and live, you'll get a fake leg. They still use peg legs today. There's even a wide one called an elephant foot.

7) I think it's the Banker who has killed Killian.

FNL

Fucking New Leg. That's what I'm getting. Janey was so excited when she found out they'd been in here today to take more measurements and that I let them. But it's still just another fake. I want the real one back. Real One. How odd that sounds. Who knows where the Real One is. I start to get mad all over again. Get out of here. Don't come back until you have the Real One.

Hop Along. Gimpy. Crip. Peg Leg. "Hey, that thing ever get termites?" "You gonna get a hook arm to match?" The list of insults and nicknames is endless. I spit out about fifty of them before I nod off, exhausted.

Sam's Back

I'm surprised when he walks through the door. Then I think he's come to announce our formal separation. Maybe a final pep talk. I turn my head and look toward the window.

Sam sits down on my bed. "I'm not that easy to get rid of," he says, smiling.

"You are if the Banker wants you gotten rid of."

"Apparently he didn't really want it then."

I can't believe that. "Are you kidding? You saw him. He was on a search and destroy mission in here."

Sam shrugs. "The heat of the moment. But I'd definitely cool it on the TV front if I were you."

I smile. "They're like bookends. They only come in pairs."

"I'll take that as a reassuring comment."

"I guess this means my afternoon isn't my own." I

sigh deeply to cover up the sudden surge of relief that tickles the back of my throat and almost makes me cough.

"Three o'clock. My office."

He's on his way out but I stop him. "You haven't seen PJ, have you?" I'm about as subtle as a train wreck, bringing up what's bothering me.

"PJ? No. She hasn't been around?"

I shake my head.

Sam says we'll talk about it some more, but I guess I know why she skittered out of the room. I was pretty hard on her the other day. All she did was pick up the new shoes. That's all. All.

Don and Doff

I'm eating all kinds of junk Coach Cutter would never let me get away with. So much for Coach Cutter. Not a single phone call. Only winners are worth his time. Forget him. Kevin, the physical therapist, is back on the scene.

"You still sore at me for tossing the leg into the whirlpool?"

"I was never the one sore," he says. "Besides, it floats. Handy if your boat capsizes. Or if your plane crashes over water."

"You're really sick."

"I know," he says, busy massaging my leg and stump with lanolin, "but please don't tell anyone. I love this job." I smile. Can't help it.

"Okay. Now, Fräulein, vee are ready for today's lesson: how to don and doff zee latest prosthesis.

Dis is how you put it don; den take it doff."

Hilarious in his mind. Ha. Bet he'd doff his lower jaw if he knew I'd already worn this clunker. Down the long long hall toward Sam's office.

Phone Call

*B*ack in my room after meeting with Sam, my head full of his words. Bits all mixed up with Kevin's stupid accent. I pour a glass of ice water and hoist myself back up on the bed. I lean forward and knock knock knock on my Rent-A-Leg. It doesn't fall off. Hasn't fallen off all day. So far so good. But it scares me a little. What if I want more?

I look toward the door. Now is the time PJ usually comes to visit. I miss her. I reach for the phone. I'll call her and apologize.

It rings with my hand on the receiver and startles the hell out of me. I tense up all over and rattle the phone in its cradle, almost drop it.

"PJ," I blurt out, "I was just going to call."

There's a long pause on the other end. A voice comes from tunnels and tunnels away. "Meghan?"

Inside I go numb. Freezer burn. It can't be. I can't

stand it to be. "Wrong number," I squeak. I hang up, slap the receiver for good measure and stare at the phone.

My hands begin to shake. My breathing goes all fast and I work to slow it down. A few seconds later the phone begins to ring again. It rings and rings. I pick it up again. "You have zee—"

Georgy cuts me off. "I know all about it and I'm coming."

"No," I shout. "Don't do that."

"You can't stop me. I want to come. I don't care what it looks like. Honest to God. Meghan, I didn't know why you weren't answering any of my letters, but now I know. It was that bruise, wasn't it?"

"Yeah." So far away and yet her voice is right here in my ear, so close it hurts.

"I'll hitchhike. Be there soon as I can."

"No. Georgy, no. Listen. It's too soon."

"I can handle it. I told you—"

"But I can't."

She pauses.

Finally I've got her attention. "I can't handle you seeing me like this."

After a few silent seconds, her voice cracks. "Oh, and I sent those shoes. How terrible that must have been."

I won't lie about that one.

"Oh, God, I'm sorry."

"I'm going to wear them, both of them. They do wonders with plastics these days." I'm starting to

238

sound like Sam. I can't believe it. "And soon as I can find a name that fits."

I can hear Georgy sniffling in the background. I feel my eyeballs start to ache. In a minute, we'll both be leaking salt water into the phone.

"Look, just don't come yet."

"Not if you don't want me to, but you can't stop me from calling."

"Okay," is all I say, though suddenly I wish I could curl up on my bed with the receiver next to me on the pillow, not talking. Just knowing that Georgy is at the other end. Maybe even sleep like that.

"Meghan, are you there?"

"I'm here."

"Don't be mad at your dad for phoning me."

"The Banker?" The shock of hearing Georgy's voice hadn't even let me wonder how she might have found out.

"I know," says Georgy. "Do you believe it?"

Holy cow. After the big blowout. And the way his eyes shot darts at both of us in the dean's office. "It's a miracle," I say.

"I guess it is." Georgy's voice cracks again but she gets it under control and keeps talking.

Before we hang up, Georgy tells me that she has all the maps, has figured out the best roads to take to get back to Springfield.

"Whenever you say so, I'll be there." Then she hangs up.

Brother Sighting

I lean over the bed, feel my hair fall and touch the floor. Blood fills my stitched lip, but nothing hurts right now. I grab the shoe box, pull it from underneath the bed. I toss the lid, yank out the tissue in the toes and shove in my hands. I walk the sneakers up the side of the bed and across my lap.

PJ comes in with her fingers cold red. Forgot her mittens. She drops her book bag on the floor, walks toward the closest chair and sits. She cups her hands to her mouth and blows. Doesn't even notice the shoes. She pulls the sleeve of her sweater over each hand like an amputee. Her cheeks are red, and the tips of her ears too. I think she is the cutest thing alive. I'm so damned glad to see her.

"PJ. I'm sorry—"

"Meghan," she says, all breathless.

"No wait. I've been a real jerk and I'm sorry."

All these words fly right by her.

"Meghan! I think I saw Killian today."

I stare at her. The words don't quite sink in. "You saw him," I repeat. "Where?"

"Right here near the hospital. You know that bus stop on the corner?"

I sit straight up on the bed and swing my leg around. "You sure it was Killian?"

"I think so. He was wearing a green army jacket. Like the one he came home with. I called to him and started running, but he got on the bus and it drove away."

I ask her a ton of questions, but that's all she can tell me. Killian so close. Close and a galaxy away.

We're silent as we share a bag of Fritos. All you can hear is the crunch of the corn chips.

Camp and Company

"You'll be happy to know, Pop," wrote Killian, "that my first meaningful job in this man's army is to stir up shit." At the dinner table I fell out of my chair laughing. I'd already read the letter, but to see the Banker's face turn red when he got to that part was just too much.

Killian had finally made it to his assigned camp, but his company was gone. Out on an operation. More endless waiting with no gun. No one had assigned him a gun. Or a place to sleep. He was with another new guy named Snoopy. While they waited for their company, he and Snoopy torched turds. Dragging fifty-five split-gallon drums out of the privies. Filling them with kerosene. Ignite and stir. Stir until it all burned away.

It was an all-day task, and smudged the air and everything around them. Not at all like the fresh horse manure Killian used to haul home for my mom's lilac bushes.

The next two days brought another prestigious job. Filling sandbags. We didn't hear from him again until the company came back to the camp.

FNG

*T*hey came out of the jungle. Bronze warriors. Covered in mud and sweat. Boots soiled red. Toting their canteens and M16s. Sores on their arms. Stubble on their faces. Gaunt. Not like any men Killian had ever seen before. Behind their eyes was something vacant and deep and Killian said they looked right through him and the other New Guys.

"Out of my way you FNG!"

Mostly, though, they ignored the New Guys. Killian was veal. Plump and clean and ignorant.

FNGs were a liability. A jinx. Cherries rot quickly. No one wants to be near them. Especially the guys getting ready to return home. To the land of the Big PX.

It wasn't long after their return that the company went out again, taking Killian and the other FNGs. Creeper with the ear necklace was a three-tour veteran. Killian was mesmerized by the shel-lacked human ears, couldn't take his eyes off of them as Creeper yanked one thing after another off of him. You need this. Not this. This. Not this. And so on. Killian's gear was packed tight. Efficient. Thanks to Creeper.

Creeper did the same for the other FNGs. That was all. You cherries rattle out there, Charlie takes notice. I don't give a shit about your hide. Bullets aimed your way come my way too.

Next, Creeper turned to Killian's friend Snoopy. You, Big Ears, you're the new radioman.

It didn't do any good to protest. You were low man. So low, said Creeper, you could do chin-ups on an ant's wiener. And so, with their gear tightly packed, the FNGs set out for their first trip into the bush. Snoopy carrying twenty-five pounds of radio and antennae. Killian with his M16 and rucksack. Inside, the low man lot of C rations. Ham and lima beans.

Shaking Hands

We had this handshake as kids. Spit into your palm. Shake your buddy's hand. Let the spit mingle and create suction. It's a done deal, sealed.

There's the dairy salesman handshake: alternately pull on the person's index and little fingers. Then there's lock-your-little-pinkies-and-repeat-a-rhyme, which you do when both of you magically happen to say the same thing at the same time. Last, there's the firm manly handshake the Banker and Killian exchanged when he came home. I still believe the udder tug would have been more intimate.

Whenever I shake hands, I do it right. Tight and firm. I hate that soft-clammy-wet-limp shake some people give you. My fingers are long and lean. My palm kind of square. It never made a very good turkey trace on grade-school Thanksgiving cards.

Killian's hands are small. In Nam, he squeezed the pus out of them every day. Making tight fists. Little leaf cuts and sores that wouldn't heal. At one point it was so bad he carried his M16 like a baby. Cradled in his arms and elbows, hands empty. His clothes, wet, worn, and dirty, began to fall off. No one wore underwear. You were less likely to get crotch rot.

I think how his small bony hands have pointed a rifle. Pulled a trigger. Ended a life. Like that. Sweet-looking fingers. Click.

After Lincoln got the presidential nomination, a sculptor made plaster casts of his hands. They weren't small. They weren't sweet-looking. But they were never used to kill. Just sore from so much hand-shaking, the right one swollen to high heaven on account of so much squeezing.

As president, Lincoln opened up the White House to folks two nights a week. He wouldn't be able to use his hand for hours afterwards. Right hand. White kid glove all streaked. Once he made the mistake of wearing unfashionable black gloves to an opera. That's all the press could talk about the next day. But by inauguration night Mary Todd made sure his gloves were the right color as he stood shaking twenty-five hands a minute.

Lincoln didn't like wearing gloves one bit. Especially when shaking the hands of old friends. Mrs. Lincoln kept giving him gloves and he kept tugging them off. Like a magician, he once pulled out seven or eight pair from his overcoat pocket. One after the other.

Glove or no glove, he would shake a soldier's hand no matter how greasy or dirty. The night of his second inaugural, he shook six thousand hands. One of those was the hand of a one-legged veteran who said to his nurse that he'd gladly lose the other leg for a man like that.

At army hospitals Lincoln shook the hands of rebel prisoners too. Strolling from cot to cot. Until his whole arm was lame from handshaking. I wish I could have shook his hand. I don't imagine one more would have tired him too much. Maybe I would hug his neck. Stand up on my toes with my heels in the air and reach way up.

Feet and Shoes

As kids we never went barefoot. Even in the soft June grass. Sandals or sneakers only. Barefoot children—a sign of parents who didn't care. About germs. About puncture wounds. About hot tar bubbles on pavement. It never occurred to me—watching them eat Sno-Kones or Mister Softees—that maybe their parents didn't have money for shoes.

In Pop Kelley's day it was different. He went barefoot a lot of times. Like Lincoln. Saved his shoes for church and school.

One Illinois winter Lincoln saw a young man he knew with rags around his feet. He was chopping logs for shoe money. Lincoln took the ax from the young man and sent him to the general store to warm up. A while later Lincoln comes in and says, "Go get your shoes."

Outside, there's wood all neatly chopped.

The Banker would make us work for new shoes. Wash the station wagon. Mow the lawn. Clean outside windows. Then I'd always be sorry. Blisters, along with the new loafers. I'd end up taking them off. Putting on my sneakers. And oxfords were worse. It took forever to break them in. Because of my tender feet.

More than once Lincoln was seen limping from new boots. Some days he'd scuff around the White House in slippers. Give his feet a chance to breathe, he'd say. As president, he had a chiropodist operate on his feet. A Jew like Sam. Doctor Cut Corns.

Foot and leg injuries were common in Lincoln's day. Sometimes they were there at birth. Famous men limped in and out of the White House: Thaddeus Stevens dragging a clubfoot, August Belmont from a bullet wound collected in a duel over a woman. General Lee had an old foot wound from the Mexican War. And at Antietam, General Hooker was blown clean off his horse when he was shot in the foot. Once near the front lines, a bullet spun past Lincoln into the ankle of a Union doctor just a couple of feet away from him.

That was nothing compared to the many soldiers who filled Washington with their missing feet, arms, eyes, and legs.

New Leg

Kevin watches as I pick it up. It's heavier than the one I'm wearing. And the ankle does funny things.

"It's the best leg on the market for athletes today," says the prosthetist.

"Buy a couple for yourself."

Both the prosthetist and Kevin ignore my snotty comment. The ankle is something else. "It's what they call multiple axis with a built-in rotator unit," the leg artist adds.

"A robot's dream come true."

"That means, Meghan, that you can tread all over uneven ground with it on." Kevin thinks he's hooked me with that line.

"So?"

"So," says Kevin, "I'm talking plowed cornfields and rocky surfaces."

"I'll be sure and take it on my next moon mission."

"Meghan, you could learn to hike Yosemite with that thing on. It takes work. I'm not saying it will be easy, but the good news is these things are only going to get better and stronger."

"And eventually lighter," says the prosthetist. "For now, it's going to be noisier, heavier, and need more repairs than the one you have on, but it's part of the athlete's trade-off."

The words barely register. For a second I picture myself walking like a real person again.

"Of course we'll need to make some minor adjustments." The prosthetist has got a whole box full of tools and gadgets. And a plastic pen case in his suit pocket full of little clip-on screwdrivers and such.

"We need to be sure you can get around on it okay," says Kevin. "The ankle is different from the rigid one you're accustomed to. It takes a little getting used to."

I don't say anything. Instead, I take the leg off of my lap and stand up. I hoist the FNL underneath my left arm, balancing the foot part behind me. I head for the door.

Mr. Pocket Protector watches me, his face looking like he's totally missed the bus. "Hey, where are you going with that leg?"

"Out the door is an improvement," Kevin says. "Last one ended up in the whirlpool."

Their voices fade behind me. I make my way slowly down the hall. In the elevator, when I reach for the button, I see that my hand is doing a little jig. The door opens and I beat a path to my room. I wedge a crutch against the door. Next, I sit in the chair with the FNL on my lap, and try to slow my breathing. In. Out. Slow. Down. Swallow dry.

I twist the ankle back and forth. I bring it to my nose and sniff it. Then I bounce it like a long skinny watermelon on my knee. Ten or twenty minutes go by. Someone knocks on my door.

"Go away."

"Are you alright?"

"Peachy."

Kevin's sneakers squeak their way down the hall.

Alone again. Just me, my leg, and the shakes. What if it doesn't work? *Step right up, folks. Be the first to see the girl with the whirling gizmo for a leg.* I stand up to go to the bathroom and pee. But I know I don't have to. I look down at the leg I'm wearing. Bend over and do the knock-knock routine again. Rent-A-Leg has about as much flexibility as a two-by-four. What do I have to lose?

I sit back down with the FNL, twist the ankle over and over. Noise. Not exactly the kind of person you'd want to sit next to in a movie theater. I swallow. It's like the Sahara in here. Up again, I walk over to the nightstand. Forget the glass. I drink right out of the stainless steel pitcher. Ice-cold water drips down my chin. I drink until it feels icy numb above my eyes. Still my throat is dry. Chocolate. I pull open the nightstand drawer, grab a Hershey's bar, tear the brown paper, and peel back the foil. Step back to the chair and sit. I chew the chocolate until my mouth is in confection heaven. Then I ball up the foil and roll it between my palms. When I get a nice bullet-sized ball, I shoot it at my Lincoln books. "Come on," I say. "I could use some company."

There's a dry sweetness in my mouth as I drop the Rent-A-Leg onto the floor. Clunk. Dead weight, good riddance. Another for the pile at Shiloh. I guide my stump into the new socket. Adjust the straps that hang from the cuff around my thigh and connect to the prosthesis. Like hitching up a horse. Giddyup. Soon enough I'm standing. Catch my breath. In. Out.

The first couple of steps I'm so anxious that I don't feel anything, not even the extra weight. One foot goes in front of the other. In. Out. I breathe a sigh of relief. Think about the bright white-and-maroon shoes waiting under my bed. The thought of the neon green laces makes me smile. I take another step. Suddenly I'm facing one way and the ankle another.

Postcard

Dear Mr. Lincoln,

Are we only parts of something? How many parts do we lose before we are part of nothing? I dreamed a dream last night. In it a quartet of singers I admire were doing a show just for me. They came out of a fog, seaweed in their hair, and singing:

Yesterday all my troubles seemed so far away.

Men in skinny ties and white jackets. They reach for me. One with big cold hands pulls off my leg. Another with rings on his fingers pulls off my arm.

Then there is laughter and one of them
starts singing:

Suddenly you're not half the girl
you used to be.

A horrible sick dream. Like your own
vision of assassination. Oh, Mr. Lincoln, I
believed in yesterday.

Your Daydream Believer,
Meghan Hartman

Snoopy

*N*icknames. Nicknames headed my way. So what's the big deal, I tell myself. Everybody has one. Especially in Vietnam. Professor. That's what they called Killian. On account of his one semester of college. The most schooling on the squad. Some didn't even graduate high school. Like Snoopy. A gung ho Georgia boy whose daddy had fought in World War II. On the shores of Iwo Jima, he almost drowned during the landing under the weight of his pack. Years later, suffocating from lung cancer, he kept saying he wished he had.

Snoopy wanted to join the marines like his daddy had, but the day he made up his mind for certain, the marine recruiter was out to lunch, and by the time he got back, Snoopy found himself all signed up with the army man instead.

His real name was Sidney but they called him

Snoopy on account of his big beagle-looking ears and long sad face. Even though he was always cracking jokes, his face was sad and lonesome, like Lincoln's. It wasn't long before Killian sent a photograph of the two of them together, Snoopy a head taller than Killian. Sure enough, you could see those huge ears sticking out of his head, and a mournful smile tugging at his face.

I know Killian must have liked him a lot to have his photo taken and to send it. Killian didn't like having his picture taken. He was funny that way.

Creeper got his name for stealth in the bush. But others said the name came from what he gave you— the creeps. Lincoln had nicknames, too. In 1830 he and a relative hired themselves out to split fence rails. Over three thousand of them. Thirty years later "Rail Splitter" would catch on and become the symbol of his candidacy for president. A symbol of the West and a humble beginning.

The nickname everyone knows: "Honest Abe," because of the fairness he showed dealing with folks beginning in his early New Salem days.

Those days the prairie grass was high, just like the open fields of Vietnam. Pioneers were sod busters. Those who broke up the hard earth. Now when you look at the fields all neat and orderly, it's hard to imagine that blood was shed there. But it was. Scalps were taken when Chief Black Hawk reclaimed land in the prairie valley. Papers he had signed tricked him. White men giving firewater to the Indians first. They burned cabins. Left shiny red spots of flesh on the heads of men and women. The size of a silver dollar.

Settlers arrived and were not wanted. The Indians were there and were not wanted. Seems there are always people in places where they are not wanted and other people ready to kill them, or herd them away because of it.

In Vietnam, it was the soldiers who were not wanted. The people fear us, wrote Killian. They despise us. But they smile. All the time they smile their brown smile.

What Legmen Carried

*P*oncho. Liner. Canteens. Flak jacket. Helmet. Entrenching tool. Steel pot. Cloth bandoliers with ammunition—about fourteen magazines. An M16 rifle. Bayonet. Frag grenades. Smoke grenades. Four pounds of C-4 plastic explosive. Five days of C rations. Foot powder. Extra socks. First aid kit. Gun oil. Towel. Knife. A small bag for personals. All this was worn, hung on web gear, or packed in a rucksack. Ninety pounds total. Thank God for Creeper, who helped lighten the load. Killian only weighed 140.

There is no measure for the invisible weight.

Kilometers, or klicks they called them. Klick after klick they walked. Carrying those packs. Sometimes fifteen or twenty kilometers a day. With all that weight. They would get up with the sun. Walk single file. Through jungle, hills, fields of high grass. Past hooches of thatch and bamboo. Sometimes larger villages. At noon they would stop and eat their C rats. Killian graduated from lima beans to spaghetti and meatballs.

After lunch, Killian could never get his pack on again without help. Sometimes he'd pull up against a tree. Or Snoopy would help him. Then they'd walk until late afternoon. Then they'd make camp. Set up a perimeter. Trade off on guard duty. Two hours on. Two off. Two on. Two off. The ground was never dry. Killian would make like a roly-poly, curl up in his poncho liner, hide from the mosquitoes and sleep his two hours.

At daybreak it was eighty degrees. They checked their weapons. Made a lousy cup of instant coffee. And started out all over again with those packs.

Killian wrote that he was always tired. Never slept more than three or four hours a night. Tired all the time. What he wouldn't give for a good night's sleep and a pair of dry socks.

Flashback

It's a hell of a night and I can't sleep. Can't read. Can't concentrate. Janey and I start a game of Scrabble, but I just stir the wood blocks, taking forever to draw.

"We'll just talk then."

That's fine with me.

Janey says, "You're struggling so hard lately. I know it's really tough."

"Tough on all us foot soldiers," I mumble.

We're both quiet. Then she says, "I know you really miss him."

"He won't come. I don't understand why."

"He'll come. But he's not the same. You can't let yourself forget that, Meghan."

"I don't care. I just want to see him."

Janey shifts in her chair uncomfortable-like. Maybe it's the baby. Maybe not. Maybe what I said made her antsy.

"He's still Killian."

"Well . . . yes and no. You saw him yourself, Meghan. You know."

"He'll work it out. He just needs time. I can wait." Or can I? For a few seconds I forgot why I'm here.

Janey stares out the window. "I couldn't wait, Meghan. I'm sorry. Not after Hawaii."

Hawaii. She's never talked about it. Sure, I've wondered plenty about what happened there, but I've never asked. Never felt I could.

Killian got a few days leave while he was in Vietnam. Some GIs went to Hong Kong. Others went to Hawaii. Janey wrote to Killian and said they should meet in Honolulu. She was in nursing school at the time but she went anyway. Cut all her classes for a week.

I remember the day she left. We were all so full of hope. Soon we'd hear firsthand how Killian really was. It was an endless week of waiting. Then we discovered she'd come back after the third day. Never called any of us.

Janey is still looking at me like she's waiting, and I hear myself asking what I never could before. "What did he look like when you first saw him?"

"He was thinner."

Now she's staring up above my head and I wonder if I shouldn't have asked. But she goes on and I stop holding my breath.

"His eyes were strange. But other than that he looked the same."

"The same," I repeat.

"Only he wasn't, Meghan. He wasn't the same at all. He looked the same but he wasn't." Her voice sounds quavery. "I should have known from the eyes. Before, they'd always reach inside, like he was seeing into you and it was okay to let him because he was doing it in a tender way."

"I know." I know the look.

"But it was something else entirely. They didn't seem to look anywhere. Like a blank page, you know. Just a stare with nothing in it. Then he'd hear a sound—the elevator bell down the hall—and he'd jump bolt upright, his eyes darting all around the room."

"He was like that when he came home, too." Eyes moving like a school of spooked minnows.

Janey puts her head down and closes her eyes. Her chin touches the end of the stethoscope slung around her neck. "July fourth weekend. I thought it would be a romantic reunion—us, watching the fireworks from the balcony overlooking the ocean. So stupid of me."

I watch her face. Her lashes dampen and I know she must still love him. Why is she telling me all this now? "Janey . . ."

"He pulled the blinds. Wrapped himself in the bedspread, but still kept shivering. I turned off the air-conditioning, but it made the fireworks even louder. Finally he ended up sleeping underneath the bathroom sink. The blanket over his head. Hugging a pillow." She lifts her head and wipes her eyes. "The next day he told me to go home."

How could you go from months of sleeping on the ground—dirty, scabby, always tired and wet from heat and fear—to clean white sheets and air-conditioning, and noises that don't mean anything. That's what Janey realized too late. How do you go from killing and watching people be killed to some kind of naked closeness. It makes my eyes tear too, to hear all this. And why tell me now?

Janey hugs me before she leaves and I can hear her sniffling and the sound of her white panty hose rubbing together as she walks down the hallway, waiting for the next shift to check on. Everything she's told me swarms around the room like an army of insects with no place to settle.

Visitor

*T*he midnight nurse has a death-white face. Her green eyes are always narrowed, like even the night lights are too bright. She comes in the room to check on me and asks if I want anything to help me sleep. I tell her no, not yet. She is a fan of Elvis. Goes to Graceland every year for her vacation and collects icons. Puts them on the table shrine in her living room. She's crazy about the Virgin Mary, too. Around her neck is a medallion to the Holy Mother.

Mary is the most famous saint. Virgin Mary. We always prayed to her as kids. Especially in May, her month. Small altars with lilacs and votive candles. You'd see them all over the neighborhood. Salve Regina. Ave Maria. Bring me a leg and I'll bring you lilacs. That's my prayer to her now.

Lincoln told a story about her. One he'd read in the newspapers. There's something in it that reminds me of me. But I'm stuck as to exactly how.

This Italian sea captain ran into a rock. Knocked a hole in the bottom of his ship. While his men were bailing out water, he went to the bow of the ship. Stood before a statue of the Virgin and prayed. The ship was sinking fast. All were sure to drown. In a fury over no heavenly help, the captain grabs the Virgin Mary. Throws her overboard. Then the leak stops suddenly and the boat makes it safely into harbor. Docked for repairs, they find the statue stuck headfirst in the hole.

I think about this and other things. It's two o'clock and I am sweating in the sheets. I finally take something from the green-eyed nurse to help me sleep but I guess I'm fighting it. I think of my fake leg, resting next to the bathroom sink. I've washed the socket, wiped it dry. There's a clean stump sock in there too. All ready to greet me in the morning. Hurray.

I toss off the sheets. I'm hungry for sugar and chocolate and toffee and anything sweet so that at least my mouth will feel good. At least that. I get up on my crutches and begin my rubber-like walk to the nurses' break room. I buy a Cat-Tail, some M&Ms, a bag of pretzels, a Hershey's bar. The door flies open and the white face says "You shouldn't be up. That's a strong sedative. Go lie down and let it work."

She tries to confiscate my candy and escort me back to bed. "Alright, I'm going. I'm going." I toss my sweets into an empty pillowcase. I've learned from these trips to the candy machine to carry one. She watches me with my pendulum walk as I slowly swing myself down the hall, too stubborn for her help. It takes a while. Even the air is starting to move a little, the way it does above a road on a hot day.

I close the door behind me. My heart thumpity-thumps when I come toward the bed and see the back of some man sitting there. "I'm sorry," I say. "I've got the wrong room."

I'm getting ready to back out but I see the dresser with the hobo and other stuff of mine. Suddenly I'm confused. Then the man turns around and I recognize his face, and say, most intelligently, "What are you doing here?"

He just kind of smiles and shows me his hands and says, "I've been gettin' all these here postcards. Thought I'd see for myself what it's all about." He gets up off the edge of the bed and he's so tall. Ceiling tall and casting a shadow that takes up the whole room. "Mind if I sit in this here *cheer* a spell."

He sits down next to the bed. I try to talk but nothing comes out. Finally I manage to say, "I know you're in my head. It's this medicine, isn't it? It's just the medicine."

"Suit yourself," he says, stretching out his legs. "But I'd say I'm a mite big to be in your head, wouldn't you?"

I just look at his long long legs and I know he's

right. "Those are some big boots."

"Yep. Taken me a long time to get 'em just the way I want 'em and then the unexpected happens."

Right away I figure he's referring to the theater night, getting shot and all, so I just kind of drop my head out of respect for the living dead or whatever he is.

"Yep," he says, "had 'em all broken in, soft in the sore spots and darn if Tad didn't hitch them to the back of his goat wagon. Pulled off both the heels." Then he laughs good and loud having got the best of me. And I laugh too, though not as loud, nervous the nurse will hear us and come in.

I sit down on the bed and put my crutches to the side. Of the hundred and one questions spinning in my brain, none slows down long enough for me to latch on to it and speak. I just look at him. Bigger than life. Those big hands dwarfing the arms of the chair. And his face. His face is a horribly beautiful thing. It takes my breath away.

"So you got a leg missing," he says. "I'm sorry about that."

"Me too." Is he going to make another joke? No, it's not in his face. "I guess you've seen a lot of those. Missing parts and all."

He pulls in his outstretched legs and sits up straight in the chair. "Too many I'm afraid. All Washington is filled with suffering. Wooden Legs. Empty sleeves. Crutches. Slings. They come hobbling

269

and crawling from battle. There are no words for young stalks so cruelly cut down."

Then he looks curiously at the crutches, leans forward and takes the top one resting against the bed. I see the scar on his thumb from an old ax wound and I know for sure it's him.

He lays the crutch across his knees and fiddles with the wing nut that connects the footpiece. "These crutches are an improvement."

"That's nothing. You should see my new leg. It's got a multiple-axis ankle with a built-in rotator unit. You can move on uneven ground with it. It's getting adjustments, but I'll have it back tomorrow." I can hardly believe my own voice, how excited I am about that damn new leg. "It's really state-of-the-art," I add.

"State-of-the-art," he repeats, like he's never heard that combination of words before. "I'd like to tinker with that." He lays the crutch to the side of his knee, asks me what's in the pillowcase.

"Candy. You want some?" I take out the Cat-Tail, M&Ms, pretzels, and Hershey's.

He's curious and looks at each one. He takes out his glasses, pulls back the tiny wires and puts them on. He turns over the M&Ms to read the ingredients.

"You don't want to know what's in all these things," I say. "Preservatives and dye and junk."

"It's a long way from dried jerky." He picks up the pretzels. "Let's try these heart-shaped things." He opens the bag. You can hear him crunching all over the room. "Not half bad for stale bread." He looks at the back of the package again, spectacles low on his nose. I guess he takes my advice because soon he takes off the glasses and puts them back in his suit pocket, not bothering to read anymore.

"PJ and I, we eat a lot of candy together. PJ is my little sister."

"I know who she is. Got all those figures in her head." He wonders if she'll ever square the circle. Says he tried after reading Euclid but it wore him out.

"Right now she's more interested in mice than math." Mouse and food gone each morning. PJ's secret soup kitchen.

He nods.

But who knows, maybe one holds the clue to the other. Like Georgy's odd connections. Popcorn and clouds. Where was I? My mind is racing.

A thought about Killian comes next but I lose it. I'm beyond tired and my head is spinning with so much excitement and when I finally grab hold of a thought it's about the theater. If all this is true and he's just caught in some momentary time warp or something, maybe I can tell him *Our American Cousin* is not that great of a play. I bring up the subject and he says. "If not the theater, some other place. What happens to us happens, Meghan."

He finishes his pretzels and says it's time for him to go. He kind of likes the crinkly clear package and asks me if he can keep it. He folds it in fourths and sticks it in his pocket when he stands up. Then he shakes my hand and says, "Run some in the cornfields for me. Don't get much of a chance to do that sort of thing anymore." Then he takes his other hand and tousles the hair on the top of my head. He disappears as he walks toward the door.

I touch my hair after he leaves and it electrifies my hand. I pick up the pillowcase, shake it again to be certain nothing is still inside. I poke at the packages on the bed. The pretzel bag is gone. I'm sure I bought pretzels. Sure.

V.
Brother

Corn

*P*opcorn. Why didn't I have popcorn instead of pretzels? That would have gotten him going, and maybe he would have stayed longer. We could have talked all night about corn. How long did he stay? He was here, wasn't he? Corn. Better to think about corn.

As a young attorney, Lincoln once tracked down a judge in a Springfield cornfield. Got documents signed for a client. Cornfield Court, the two men called it, laughing at themselves.

I laugh at myself. Maybe because I'm going crazy. First my leg. Now my mind. I'm in short supply of everything. No short supply of corn here in the heartland though. Sure wasn't in Lincoln's time either, though back then they only got twenty bushels of corn to an acre. Today we get over one hundred and twenty. Why didn't I think to mention that? I didn't ask one-tenth of the questions popping in my head like bingo balls.

The first ball comes up:

I, 12. Indian corn, a dozen varieties. I wonder if they hung Indian corn on the door in Long Legs' time. These days, the whole neighborhood's in on it. Even the downtown stores. It's a colorful decoration but no good to eat. Mostly what's grown around here is field corn, no good eating either, unless you happen to be a chicken or a cow.

R, 2. Reality. Are there two kinds? More than two? Was he really here? How many Killians are there? Did the Banker really call Georgy? Scarce visitor at the hospital. Here day and night at first. Firing Sam. Hiring him back. A mistake maker. A mistake fixer. Buyer of televisions. Some mistakes can't be repaired. But then, maybe some can.

P, 8. Pretzels. He ate the pretzel proof. I read somewhere if you think you're going crazy, you're fine. It's only when you're sure you're fine that you're probably crazy. Better to think about corn. Corn country grows some fine things for us two-legged creatures too. Gardeners here plant all kinds that mature at different rates. That way they can eat corn all summer long. You start planting when oak leaves are no bigger than a squirrel's ear. You can plant Golden Beauty. Early Sunglow. Both yellow varieties. There's a white-and-yellow mix that comes later. Honey and Cream. Butter and Sugar. Pearls and Gold.

S, 9. Asinine. It is asinine to believe he was really here, isn't it? But he was. Why bother finishing the report when you've met the man?

Yellow hybrids are popular to can or freeze. Illini. Seneca Chief. Still, my favorite to eat are the white hybrids, tiny and sweet. And the best of all in my opinion is the Silver Queen. Cook it the day it's picked and you'll think you died and went to heaven. Corn is like God in this county; it's everywhere and people swear by it.

H, x^n. Heaven. Variable unknown. Not on bingo card. Try turning card over.

PJ. Corn. My first memory of PJ eating corn. She had just lost her two front teeth around the time of first harvest. She left a corkscrew trail winding all the way around the cob. It's odd how little things like that stick in the brain. To think of people as snapshots. Frozen like a box of corn in a moment of time.

G, 63. Gettysburg. 1863. That picture of his face breaks my heart. I wish I had given him more than just an empty pretzel package.

Killian

It's late when he comes. I'm sitting on the bed reading all about Mr. Lincoln's prairie years. A small cone of yellow light shines from the lamp. I don't notice him until he softly clears his throat. How could I have not heard his footsteps? I've been listening for them for so long. He seems so small and tired-looking. Not at all like my memories.

His army jacket swallows him. It's dark green and dirty. He stands there, hands in pockets. I'm surprised to see him and I'm not surprised. I knew—wanted to believe—he would come. But seeing him like this, Brother Bones, I just don't know.

"What are you reading there, Meghan?" he asks.

"Just a book on Lincoln." I close it with my finger in the middle and hold up the spiny edge, trying to keep it from shaking.

He walks closer to the bed of light. There's an

odor of grease, old bacon grease. I see that his Levi's are dirty too. Where does he sleep? What does he eat? He leans forward, squints to read the title but keeps his hands in his pockets, which is very unlike him.

"Oh, the Sandburg, that's a good one," he says.

"Yeah," I echo, "it sure is."

Killian never used to be able to resist touching books. He always said that his first job, his job at the library, was the best he'd ever had. Sometimes the librarian would find him lost in the stacks. He'd be sitting on the floor, caught up in one of the books he was supposed to have reshelved. I could always tell when he'd been at the library because he came home with a paper smell on his clothes and a spacey look in his eyes.

"You reading all those others, too?" He points with his green canvas elbow to the books on the nightstand.

"They're for a report I was going to do for school." I wonder how he got in. It's way past visiting hours. Then again, given last night, why bother asking how people get into this place. I don't care how. I'm glad he's here. Wish he'd sit down.

Killian looks from the books to the drawn curtains to the dresser—anywhere but at me and the empty leg space. I watch him as he moves beyond the light toward the small dresser. He takes his hands out of his pockets and picks up the small hobo. He cranks the musical knob on the wooden base and Johnny begins spinning circles to the old raindrops tune.

Killian watches the little statue turn. "Good old Jerry the tramp."

"Jerry?" I'm startled. I can't believe he doesn't remember. All the stories Pop Kelley told us. How could he forget poor Johnny. Simple Johnny, who lived for breakfast. "It's Johnny, not Jerry."

Killian shrugs, still watching the hobo.

"Killian, you want to see my FNL?" I tell him what it stands for and he laughs. It's not as full and rich of a laugh as before, but in its thinness I love it all the more. "It's in the bathroom," I say, "all cornstarched and ready to wear tomorrow morning."

He walks to the open door and flips on the bathroom light. I don't know what he sees or thinks he sees, but he flips the switch right off and turns around.

"It's not my permanent one," I explain, "but I can put it on anyway, and show you how good I get around."

"That's okay, Meghan." He walks back toward the bed and sits down in the chair next to it. Finally.

Now he is close enough that his long lashes can almost reach out and tickle my face. Why won't he hug me? Does it look that bad? Just a jigsaw puzzle missing one piece. Maybe it's him he's worried about. The smell. I don't care. Maybe I do. He can't remember Johnny and he smells like fermenting pork—all the more reason to hug me.

"How've you been, Killian?" I say. "We all miss you. I miss you."

He's quiet for a few seconds, thinking about what to say. "I can't come home just yet, Meghan."

"I know. But it's so cold out there." I try not to think of him freezing in his sleep.

"For a while it was cold everywhere," he says, "but now I don't feel it very much. Just keep walking and moving. Alive and moving."

Killian and me. It's all too much. I feel a freezer burn starting to happen. I catch my breath and say, "We had some days as kids, didn't we?" The words are nice and tender and help me catch my breath.

"We did," he says, "some very fine ones."

I think of the ice pond. That day I started to love Killian more than a sister ought to love a brother. I knew it even then. Not so much because he rescued me, but because he did it without a second thought. And because of how much he hated to fight. Then I think of all the summers pedaling our bicycles out to the lake. "You remember the lake?" Who could forget our special place, our secret Grass Lake? "You remember, Killian, what you said that day of the catfish sighting?"

"Catfish?" He's thinking hard, like he really doesn't remember, like it's all been washed from his mind, clean as a blackboard on Friday.

"The big catfish on the bottom, remember? You

said it weighed as much as a Black Angus. Would have set a 4-H record."

Killian starts to laugh his thin little laugh again and I see his teeth are a mossy yellow. Little-boy teeth so old-looking and out of place. I think about a dozen teeth things at once. Pop Kelley's teeth in my cigar box and Killian's old, boy teeth, how I would still want one if he ever left us. Just a tooth to string on a memory necklace. All the old bones of people I love would rattle around on that necklace and talk to me, and when I die I'll be buried wearing it so that all our bones can clank, bang, and knock around together and say all the things we never could say to each other while we were alive.

I think a quick prayer to Apollonia, the patron saint of teeth, whose own were smashed and broken before she was burned alive. Then I look at Killian's teeth again and remember how fine and white they were that day of the big catfish sighting. How his smile seemed to shine like the bright points of sun on the water. But since Vietnam they have turned dingy, not so different from the stained betel-nut teeth of the Vietnamese.

"Oh, Meghan, you still believe that catfish tale."

The words surprise me. "What do you mean? You said it was there. I saw it," I say, "sort of." The big dark mass at the bottom.

"Tires, Meghan. Nothing but old tires."

"You lie."

"Go see for yourself."

But I don't want to see. "Why tell me now?" I demand.

"I don't know," he says. "I guess because we're not kids anymore."

It's not like I can drive, drink, and vote. Or even join the army. "What are we then?"

"We're cherries," he says. "Picked before our time."

What can I say to that? Nothing. The music from the hobo stops.

There is quiet until I cannot bear the weight of it and so I say, "This cherry has new running shoes." I pull the box out of the lower nightstand drawer and hand it to him. He takes the lid off slowly, crinkles back the tissue paper and lifts out a shoe.

"What a beaut."

"Yeah, they're really swell."

"What are you going to name them?"

"Hop-alongs. What do you think?"

He half smiles. "I think that's a good name, Meghan."

"You think I can make 'em live up to their new name?"

"And then some. Your next pair will be Skip-alongs, and then Run-alongs."

"That's what I hope for." I'm surprised that I mean it. "I used to not, but now I do." Sebastian— the one who collected all those torso arrows around

300 A.D.—is the patron saint of athletes, but there is no saint for runners. So I voted for my own. Another third-century saint. A Greek named Conon. Spikes were driven through his feet. Then he was made to run in front of his own chariot, as men whipped him like a horse. He was an old man, so it didn't take too long for him to keel over. I guess you could say he was sort of a Hop-along too before he moved at the speed of angels.

Killian puts the shoe back in the box and slides it underneath the chair he's sitting in. That's when I get a good look at his hands. Small red scars.

Mosquitoes. Thousands of them. Laying their larvae in the rice paddies and elephant grass. Swarms hatching, rising in the heat. Thick as black clouds. High drone of attack. Laying their thin stingers into any flesh they could find. Army mosquito repellent gave Killian sores. Red blotchy ones. So he threw it away and got eaten alive. The leeches were worse. The flies, they were just a nuisance.

"I'm glad you came." I look up at his face.

"Me too. I can't stay much longer though."

"I know. The walls."

"I tried to come sooner."

"I know. PJ saw you." But she didn't tell me how bone thin he looks. "You hungry? I've got a stash."

He tells me he got something earlier at the Salvation Army, the Church of the Kitchen Implement. Soup. That is the extent of help. *Onward Christian sol-*

diers marching off to war. Only to come home like Killian. Believing in nothing. Sweet Cross of Jesus. Purple Heart. Why can't he just lean forward? Why can't we hug each other? I would give my other leg to make him whole again. There is nothing else I have to give. No, nothing. No. But a leg.

There was a peg-leg general at Gettysburg who laughed when he took a bullet in his wooden leg. And I think about the soldier who played the violin for the better part of an hour as his leg was being sawed off. A heap of parts: Feet. Legs. Arms. Hands. Walt Whitman saw a pile of them at Rappahannock. Enough to fill a one-horse cart. But what about wounds that don't show? Like Killian's?

Killian's restless and getting ready to go. He keeps glancing at the open door.

"I've got something for you before you leave." From the top drawer of my nightstand I take out my cigar box, lift up the lid with the three Dutchmen. Inside are my treasures: letters, photos, trinkets. I rearrange things until I find the silver dollars—all six of them from the late 1800s. Big and beautiful like the country used to be back then. I hand them to Killian.

"Willard's pawnshop will give you a good price for these."

For a moment I think he won't take them, but he needs them, and finally he does.

"Wait," I say. "I've got an arrowhead in here

someplace. It's a fine point and you could probably get something for that, too."

I dig around in the box and feel I am going to cry but I keep looking anyway even though it's cloudy. Cloudy. That's all. I won't let myself get beyond that.

Then Killian puts his hand on mine and says, "No, Meghan. This is plenty."

I stop right there to feel his hand on mine. Warm and scarred but still fine. We stay like that for a few seconds—me sitting on the bed and him standing there with his hand on mine. Then he slowly takes it away and pokes around in the cigar box until he finds the picture of him and Snoopy Big Ears.

He traces Snoopy's outline with his finger and says, "Some guy, that Snoopy."

"I'm sorry about what happened to him." Being a radioman, you might as well have a bull's-eye painted on your chest.

"He was good," says Killian.

He moves the photo gently aside and a tape-stained Polaroid appears. He's looking at the dead soldier—his first kill—before I can even get it out of the box. He asks me if he can have it back.

"You don't need the reminder."

"Yes. I do."

"Then you should have it."

He takes the photograph and quietly slides

it into his pocket without looking at it again. He stumbles onto Pop Kelley's teeth next. He picks them up and rattles them in his hand like a pair of dice. The teeth play a melody. The past talking, and I realize that I don't even know what Lincoln's teeth were like. Another thing I didn't pay attention to. No photographic evidence, either. Long exposure times back then, so no one smiled. Not even the grave examiners mentioned his teeth on their numerous pryings. All I know is that Lincoln once complained of a horrible toothache. Lasted days. Wonder if he knew about Saint Apollonia.

The teeth stop. Killian opens his fist and stares at them. "The Banker has a birthday coming up soon. You ought to have these made into cuff links for him." He drops them back into the box, says it's time for him to go.

He doesn't hug me. I don't think he knows what that is anymore. I try to remember where I read that love is as terrible as an army on the march.

Killian walks to the door. Thin green stalk that he is. Ready to vanish forever like my leg. But I won't let him. Not yet.

"Wait. I need you to mail something for me." I hand him the stack of postcards. A rubber band around the middle. No stamps. Long Legs has already read them. Now they're Killian's.

He looks at the top one and shakes his head in a knowing way.

"I left a little bit of room for you to write on them too, if you want."

Killian slides the postcards into his pocket and the heavy coins ting against each other. The radiator kicks on near the window, blowing hot air into the curtains as he leaves. Paper stalks rustling in his wake. It's nothing. Nothing but the muffled sound of applause fading in the distance.

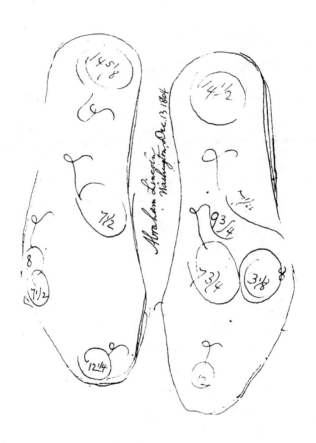